Providence Place

Matthew Tait

'Welcome to Providence Place, a long abandoned school, where some souls are yet to graduate. Not only does Matthew Tait apply his deft prose to the haunted genre, but also adds a dash of metaphysical consideration, as prevalent in his works such as *Dark Meridian* and *Olearia*. Tait offers more than a simple trip through the ghost house. A well-paced, intelligent, and deliciously dark tale.'

-Daniel I Russell, author of *Entertaining Demons*

Providence Place

Cover Art: Greg Chapman
Layout: Shannon Gambino
ISBN 10: 0-646-97697-4
ISBN 13: 978-0-646-97697-6

First Printing: October 2017

For the students and staff of Pultney Grammar

ALSO BY MATTHEW TAIT

GHOSTS IN A DESERT WORLD

DAVEY RIBBON

SLANDER HALL

DIFFERENT MASKS: A DECADE IN THE DARK

DARK MERIDIAN

OLEARIA

TABLE OF CONTENTS

At night, in schools, a transformation takes place. In effect, they are no longer schools. The bustle has left; the light has gone; the energy has been reduced to nothing.

Of course, this could be said about any building where the business of life is conducted during daylight hours ... but places of learning are a world unto themselves. Darkness descends, and they are peeled back to reveal a lifeless abode of stark hallways, quiet classrooms, and shadowy recesses that give a curious insight into the human condition – a world that is a metaphor for life itself: the human has its day; its season, then ultimately the lights go out again. In opposition, the walls and foundations stand long after the children and educators disappear. They are permanence in place of impermanence. And through the many layers of chalk-dust, through all the finger-smeared lockers, stairwells and hallways, time moves at a different speed.

The lifetime of one child is but a day in the life of a school.

ONE

Providence Place stood on the fringes of Cranston, three miles from the heart of that bustling metropolis. Officially abandoned in 2004 (immediately in the aftermath of a massacre), the entire school had been earmarked for demolition for over twelve years now. Although there were many motives for inaction in this area – budgetary and political dickering alike – it could be said the real reason for the school's continued existence was more psychological than anything else.

Or so Dillion Cook believed.

Staring at it across the parking lot (thankfully behind the wheel of his Ford Explorer), it was even easier to believe other forces were at work here: that perhaps the school itself did not *want* to be put out of commission. Composed entirely out of the same materials as every other old building in the nation, sentience seemed to cling to its windows and arches like a life-force itself, giving the front façade the mock-up intelligence of a face. There were balustrades and there were turrets; there were balconies and barbs. Immediately on the grounds below, weeds had sprung up to form a canopy of jungle and vines. While the overarching color of the stone was purple, the riot of rot now secreted into the building had given everything a charcoal hue almost devoid of color itself; as if Providence Place were the aftermath of a large-scale gravestone rubbing, its protrusions and depressions bled of solidity by the scouring of time.

And that's just the front of the school, Dillion thought, and then jumped when the passenger door of his Ford sprung open on its hinges.

Although Alyssa Asterious was entirely expected, Dillion's heart hammered at a furious pace. Only now did he become fully aware just how much this school consumed him. Visually, of course – this was a given taking into account its arresting gothic ambiance. But in every other detail as well: Providence Place was a subject Dillion had obsessed and studied for just shy of two years.

'I'm early, I know,' Alyssa said, slamming the door in her wake. Despite the chill outside she wore little more than a black t-shirt and jeans. 'But I wanted to have a word with you before the others get here.'

Dillion wasn't surprised. Having spent a good portion of her life as an actress in a variety of mediums, Alyssa was prone to rehearsals. Not just before a show … but on the real-life stage as well.

'I thought we'd –'

'Yes, we've covered everything. I signed your contract, didn't I? There's just one thing in it I'm not sure about. I'll follow you in; I'll even give you all the running commentary you need when we get inside the theater. But that's the end of the line for me. I simply won't go into those dressing rooms, and you cannot make me.'

Alyssa was talking ... but her core attention was reserved for the school, a dark pile of frowning brick the length of a football field away from the parked car. Her eyes were cagey, panicked around the edges. They were the wary eyes of someone weighing the chances of an animal turning feral.

She didn't sleep a wink last night, Dillion thought. *Besides that one visit to Providence Place for her magazine story, this is the first time she's set foot on the grounds since she was a student here.*

For a moment the reality of this pilgrimage hit home in ways he hadn't experienced. They were doing this. They were really *doing* this.

'I'm okay with that,' he said by way of reply. Except he wasn't. Not really. He could placate Alyssa for now, of course. But once inside it might be a different story. 'I'm more than grateful you've decided to return at all. I mean, after what you experienced, after what you saw inside those dressing rooms ...'

'Save it,' Alyssa told him. 'For your film and website. You don't need to play the tour guide with me.'

'Take it easy. I'm just letting you know I'm grateful.'

'Let's get one thing straight, Dillion. I'm here for the paycheck. A girl's gotta eat.'

Suitably rebuked, Dillion began the process of inspecting his equipment. He'd been over it all dozens of times, of course – but one final inventory wouldn't hurt. In addition to his personal iPhone, his backpack came equipped with three more. If for any reason one camera should fail, there were additional ones to pick up the slack. High-powered LED flashlights (five of them) poked their circular tops through the side-pockets. Food staples and energy drinks shared space with his laptop, notebooks, and an extra jacket should the temperature suddenly decide to plummet.

Because this isn't a cheap-ass ghost tour, he thought randomly. *This is supposed to be the real thing.*

Yes ... it was *supposed* to be. The motherlode of all hauntings that would finally pay dividends for Dillion's little production company. And this time he had a whole cadre of in-the-know support for the whole undertaking: men and women both who had been embedded in the front lines of Providence Place across the span of generations.

'I think I see Jeff,' Alyssa said. 'Looks like he's already been for a look-see.'

A shadow, one almost midget sized, emerged from the right of the main building. It came over slowly all the while snatching furtive, backward glances at the dilapidated locker area it had left behind. Soon the shadow resolved itself into a squat, elderly black man wearing a sizeable trench coat.

Jeff Wolfe.

As one of the janitorial staff serving at Providence Place during the school's peak heyday, Jeff had cleaned nights on the premises for close to five years. A private school catering to some of Cranston's semi-elite, the faculty did not want its cleaners immediately visible after the final bell tolled for the day. Hence their duties were often carried out under the collar of night, with classrooms emptied and hallways cleared. Jeff had told stories pertaining to Providence Place, many of them – and he was one of the few individuals to have gone public with his more outlandish encounters.

Recruiting him for tonight's misadventure had not proved difficult.

A blast of frigid air entered the Ford as the retired cleaner hopped into the back seat. Accompanying the wind was an acute smell of tobacco, cheap cologne, and stale coffee.

Rubbing his hands together, Jeff said, 'Can you believe there isn't so much as a lick of graffiti on those lockers? Even the vandals have the good sense to stay away from this place.'

'I can believe it,' Alyssa said.

'You aren't apprehensive about going in there by yourself?' Dillion asked him. 'I thought we agreed to do this thing together.'

Jeff sucked back spit, a vacuum created by the absence of a front tooth. 'You forget how long I worked here, Mr. Dillion. I know Providence Place like the back of my hand. Every nook and cranny is familiar to me.'

'Lucky you,' Alyssa said. 'Oh look, here comes a third lamb to the slaughter.'

A red Honda Civic (bearing only one occupant) had entered the carpark and idled toward the waiting Ford. With no line markers remaining on the asphalt – twelve years of weather erosion had obliterated all that once was – the Honda parked at a severe angle directly adjacent to Dillion's vehicle. By now the driver was entirely visible to them: a blond man in his thirties sporting a bowl haircut and wearing a tie.

'He the altar boy?' Jeff asked from the backseat. 'What's he doing all dressed up like that?'

Dillion had pulled out one of his notebooks and was busy flipping it to Jason Wedle's handwritten profile. 'He's not dressed up. That's just the way he is. You should probably both know that Jason is still very much a Christian boy. Getting him along for this ride wasn't an easy thing for me.'

'I'll bet,' Alyssa said. 'Poor boy still has a carrot up his ass.'

'Go easy on him,' Dillion told her. 'I don't think Jason's ever fully recovered from what happened here.'

Alyssa cackled, a manic sound. 'Have any of us?'

All three of them jumped perceptibly when Jason slammed the door of his Civic. Ambling over, he did what both Alyssa and Jeff had done before him: snatch surreptitious glances at the school while he walked. No doubt there were a whole gamut of old memories graphing themselves to the present moment.

The passenger door opposite Jeff opened, and Jason Wedle slumped in. Though over a week had passed since their first meeting together (Dillion making the trip up to Jason's house equipped with selling points on why he should return to the school in addition to a large check), Jason wore the same attire ... and the same haunted look. Over the intervening years since leaving, each individual had lived their lives trying to erase Providence Place from their memory. But then Dillion Cook had come barreling in, waving an offer of money around, and suddenly it was like they had never left. Jason, with bags under his eyes so prominent they looked like black fruit, appeared also not to have slept since the amateur filmmaker had made his offer. For a moment there was only silence; Dillion sitting in a stew of mild self-recrimination. He'd paid these individuals, yes – had given them an opportunity to put some much-needed closure on their lives. But what would the final price be after the event?

Jason cleared his throat. 'Am I the last one here, or –'

'Just one more to go,' Dillion said. 'Carolina Gates. A student from 1988 until 1991.'

'The virgin,' said Alyssa wistfully.

Dillion shifted uncomfortably in the driver's seat.

'Yes, I suppose you *could* say that.'

Through the review mirror Dillion saw Jason turn pink, an unspoken question on his lips.

'Carolina Gates,' Alyssa stated matter-of-factly, happy to inform him. 'Was a gifted swimmer for her school. She spent nights, weekends, and any free time she had doing freestyle laps in the natatorium. All with the hope for championship glory and eventually getting a scholarship to Brown University. The kids called her walrus, in reference to her buck teeth and dyke, I mean *amazing*, physique. On one particular morning when the walrus was swimming alone, something physically attacked her in the pool.'

A mild guffaw came from Jeff; Dillion couldn't tell if the man was agreeing with the statement or pouring scorn on it. Jason was staring intently at Alyssa's headrest, his fascination unalloyed.

'Anyway, she made a big splash about it – pun intended. Told anyone who cared to listen there was some kind of evil force prowling the school. Though she didn't have any evidence to back it up, of course. Not then. All that came later.'

Almost unconsciously Dillion riffled through his notebook until Carolina's profile made itself known. Like Jeff's, hers came equipped with newspaper clippings. Along with the tabloid-style headline on one article was a picture of Carolina herself, holding her heavy-with-child stomach and staring into the camera lens with a despondent frown.

Alyssa had produced a cigarette from somewhere, and she lit it before continuing. 'Whoever attacked her … knocked her up.' She held the smoke, blew it back out. 'Only a few short months after the attack she was showing, and a few months after *that* she gave birth. What made the whole thing so damn hilarious was Carolina's claim she'd never done the deed with anyone before. Like, ever.'

'She was … raped?' Jason asked.

Alyssa shook her head. 'Depends on how you look at it. Could have just been one of the dunderheads on the athletics team didn't use any protection and she was ashamed of the whole thing. But I don't think so. Carolina claimed it was a ghost who got inside of her.'

There was another muted silence, punctuated by heavy breathing from all four of them. Finally Jeff said: 'What happened to her kid?'

'She put it up for adoption as soon as it arrived. And get this –'

At the back of the Ford, something rapped against the boot. Another collective jump went through the car. Turning around, they watched on as the object of their conversation smiled at them through the back window and held up one hand in a wave.

Dillion said, 'Move over into the middle please, Jason.'

As Jason obliged, the door opened and Carolina Gates saddled herself inside. She was a large woman, bordering on obese, and Jason sat wedged between her form and Jeff's with his shoulder blades hunched and wearing a blush. Since the media event of her virgin birth, Carolina had gone on to sire three more children, all of them her own. Perhaps predictably, she'd never held steady employment – had, in fact, stayed completely inactive for going on twenty-five years now. After the furor of her story had abated, addiction to pain killers had ensued, and subsequent to that: agoraphobia. Some doctors had surmised the current state of Carolina's mental health and the swimming pool attack at Providence Place were in no way related to each other … but Dillion figured the odds against coincidence here would produce a number larger than the stars in the sky.

'I caught a bus,' Carolina informed them, and then proceeded to go about the introduction process. When Alyssa's turn came around, the woman pitched her cigarette out the window and produced an awkward, muffled greeting in reply. From her body language alone, there could be little doubt Alyssa had belonged to the 'walrus' brigade of name-callers. Whether Carolina remembered her or not was anybody's guess.

No doubt we'll soon find out, Dillion thought. *Time to get this freak-show on the road.*

'We'll begin in the main courtyard,' Dillon said, breaking what was already an uncomfortable silence.

9

'Where the fish pond used to be … or is. I have no idea if it's still there or not. I'd like to get a shot of all of you against the backdrop of the administration building.'

'Oh, it's still there all right,' said Jeff. 'Everything is. The way the school was abandoned, it was like the rapture just swept through on a normal day.'

Dillion continued as if the janitor had not spoken. 'Then we'll head over to the chapel. Is everybody ready? Alyssa, did you bring a jacket? Some parts will be cold.'

By way of reply his passenger merely held up her packet of Lucky Strikes, as if this were the only armor she required. In the back seat, Jason's reddened features had departed entirely, his cheeks now visibly pale. Carolina and Jeff continued to stare at the school, their brows furrowed in a collective arc of concentration.

Pulling out his iPhone, Dillion hit the record button.

'Okay,' he said. 'Time to do this.'

TWO

During his years of avant-garde filmmaking, Dillion had researched (and visited) his fair share of abandoned porn. The term – loosely coined almost a decade ago – described the photography taken by intrepid wanderers to the lost and derelict places of the world: cities, islands; even entire shopping centers completely abandoned to time. While the Russian city of Chernobyl often took the prize as one of the more notorious voids, Dillion had been astounded to learn almost every niche had some forgotten realm almost completely devoid of humanity and left to rot. There were amusement parks and apartment blocks; there were brothels and boiler rooms; prisons, car factories, dilapidated farmhouses painted brown with primordial blood on killing room floors. These places were grotesque, but they were also sublimely beautiful; a haunting education pertaining to mortality and time. All places, everywhere, were ruined vistas simply waiting to happen.

Yet nothing had quite prepared Dillion Cook for

Providence Place.

They stood in the central courtyard: three former students, a former janitor, and one filmmaker from another state. Although an open area, the main courtyard was an oppressive square ringed by five other crumbling buildings. To their left, one of the school's gyms; to their right, the canteen and kitchens.

To think ... this place once played host to hundreds of frolicking children playing games of basketball.

The courtyard itself was unadulterated chaos. A massive waste receptacle, usually trundled in at the end of a school year, sat perched in the center like a marooned sea vessel. Inside lay all manner of detritus: moldering work desks, sporting equipment, and even whole sinks presumably ransacked from one of the restrooms. There were exercise books and ceiling fans, broken doors and entire closets. On a large mound of old-fashioned computer screens, something moved … and it took Dillion a moment to comprehend exactly what he was looking at: a large rat, fat with liveliness, stared at them fearlessly across the refuse.

'Jesus H. Christ,' Alyssa said. 'Would you look at all this shit.'

Training his camera away from the trash, Dillion's screen alighted on the third building walling the yard: a two-story edifice once supporting elementary school classrooms. Each level, both encased in filth and grime, were now a repository for even more flotsam and jetsam – things that would be deemed alien in any school: shopping carts and mobility walkers, rusted refrigerators and hulking air-conditioners. Jeff, seemingly hypnotized by these items, had wandered over to the stairs.

'People have been using the school as a dump?' he asked nobody. 'Just how in God's name did most of that stuff get up there?'

Dillion had no answer for this. Some of the objects (like the mammoth-sized church bell) were placed on the balcony as if a giant's hand had simply positioned it on the second floor. Too cumbersome to be transported by the staircase (or by other means immediately evident), Dillion could only surmise an industrial crane had done the work. Why anyone would desire such a thing for the bell's final resting place was the biggest mystery of all.

'Oh God, no.'

The voice belonged to Jason, who was standing with his back to them and inspecting the outdoor fish pond. Artificial and rectangular (a joint project of the middle school students), the communal pond had once housed common Shubunkins in addition to a variety of turtles. Or so Dillion had read. Though information regarding the school's history was sometimes hard to come by, there were still a few websites devoted to unearthing its mysteries.

Carolina and Alyssa had joined him, and together they stood staring down into the pond as if the secrets of the universe were etched there.

'What is it?' Dillion asked.

His camera found the oddity first.

A solitary fish (one large Shubunkin) swam languidly in three feet of crystal clear water. Weeds, densely packed tendrils of them, floated their tips just above the surface. Dillion could even smell the malodorous stink of the pond itself: a gamey reek of sewage and groundwater.

Unconsciously stroking his tie, Jason said, 'Somebody's been here, cleaning this thing and keeping it functioning.'

'And feeding the fish,' Carolina added.

Through the screen of his iPhone, Dillion zoomed in on the lone inhabitant of the pond. Physically healthy, there could be little doubt the Shubunkin dined as regularly as the rat. Despite the ruinous state of the courtyard itself, animal life appeared to be thriving.

Bending down, Alyssa gently placed an index finger into the water.

'Careful,' Jason said. 'What are you doing?'

'Just testing is all. Seeing if it's real.'

She stood back up, brought her nose to the tip of her finger. 'What? Have you forgotten Providence Place has been branded a notorious hot spot for the supernatural? Isn't this the main reason why we're here? Who's to say whether this pond is … natural.'

'Good point,' Dillion said, and then bent down himself. Although he didn't deign to touch the water. 'Everything here sure feels real. You can hear the gurgling sound of the pump beneath the reeds.'

Carolina said, 'Lacking a few more residents, I bet this is just how the pond looked at its peak.'

No one replied, preferring instead to simply stare down at the water and frown. The sun, already obscured by low-level clouds, had finally dipped beyond the horizon. A grey soot stain had invaded the courtyard, transforming the already Cimmerian atmosphere bleaker still. For a moment, Dillion felt a pang of anxiety brought on by the sheer unknown that lay ahead. Of course, they had no permit to come here, and the grounds themselves were off limits to the public at large. Besides the four present, he had informed only one other person of his pet-project, preferring instead to keep the entire thing under wraps until he had some decent footage and paid for an appropriate domain name. What if something were to go wrong or one of them injured themselves traversing this muck? No insurance – and certainly no compensation policies – existed for a piddling production company dealing with the paranormal.

'What's wrong, Dillion?' Alyssa asked. 'You look lost.'

'Nothing,' he said. Standing up, he tried to project a calm assurance. 'All of you – if you could walk over to the dumpster and stand in a horizontal line please. And … try to look serious.'

'The money shot?' said Jason.

'I think that's supposed to come later,' Jeff answered.

Doing as instructed, all four gathered in a loose knot by the receptacle. Carolina, completely self-conscious now the camera was out, had taken to smoothing out her bulky flower-print dress with nervous energy. Jason's eyes remained fixated on the southern end of the courtyard, their next stop and where the hidden chapel lay in wait.

Running his iPhone through a variety of apps, Dillion had managed to find an agreeable backdrop where decent light prevailed. 'Alyssa, could you at least wait until we're finished to light up please? I don't want this looking like an advert for Lucky Strikes.'

'And just what are *you* doing? Filming your whole

project on a freaking iPhone? I bet you're one of those sad - sacks who camp out for days waiting for their next hit of tech.'

Taking a long, slow drag of her cigarette, Alyssa stared at Dillion as if mounting a challenge. Ever the pacifist, Dillion chose not to prompt her further. Let her smoke – he could work with that. It all added to the crestfallen quality of his cast.

When they were suitably lined up, Dillion spoke into his phone.

'Twelve years ago, unimaginable tragedy befell Providence Place – an upper-class Rhode Island school of over seven hundred fulltime students. A lone gunman opened fire on one of three chartered school buses as it pulled into the rear parking lot to drop off children. Four students died that day, all of them pupils under the age of fifteen. This was the catalyzing event that brought Providence Place into the mainstream consciousness. But what many people do *not* know is the calamity that day was only an epilogue in a long line of misfortunes … malevolent incidents that have been going on here ever since the original trustees met to establish the school in 1847. There have been accidents, and there have been suicides. In 1990, a high school junior, Carolina Gates made local headlines by claiming she was attacked while training for the upcoming state freestyle swimming championships. Alyssa Asterious's encounter in the theater has also been well documented. Apparitions have always been a constant, everything from moving shadows in the corridors to the presence of unknown children who briefly appear only to disappear again.'

Sudden cackling broke the monologue, and Dillion looked away from the screen to find the drama student herself grinning into the camera. 'I'm sorry,' she said, but continued to snigger, one hand clamped over her mouth. 'It's just that you sound like that guy who does those honest trailers.'

Dillion thumbed the camera off, barely managing to hold back a rising tide of anger. In the real world, Alyssa Asterious was boisterous and opinionated; he'd garnered this insight and more after their first meeting together. But he had also paid her handsomely for her presence here; the *least* she could do was afford him some respect while filming.

'If looks could kill,' she said, grinding out what remained of her cigarette. 'I apologize, okay? Just trying to cope with this situation in my own weird way. Please continue, Dillion.'

'Forget it. I'm done for now anyway.' Reaching down, he reclaimed his backpack and re-shouldered it. 'It's time for all of us to head over to the chapel.'

At the words his cast remained motionless, standing stupidly by the dumpster as if only now becoming aware of their true surroundings. Although full dark was still more than an hour away, their collective silhouettes were but charcoal smudges in the gloom, each individual incorporated perfectly with the debris behind them. Finally, as if awakening from a fugue state, the four silently made their way over to where Dillion waited.

Walking as one, they covered the rest of the distance to the chapel, one doorway among many into the greater heart of Providence Place.

THREE

Caking the pews and festooning the carpet, mold grew like a strain of algae over every surface and wall of what had once been a place of worship.

Playing over the fungus, five separate flashlight beams illuminated a high ceiling festooned within a network of spider webs traversing biblical friezes. The church's many pews (stadium-like stalls arching down diagonally to the main pulpit) formed a wide circumference of vandalized seat cushions whose stuffing lay exposed like disgorged innards. And littered among this stuffing: dozens of small, leather-bound books – what Dillion could only assume were decaying copies of the New Testament.

'This isn't how I remember it,' Jason said from behind the group. The timid man stood well back in the shadows of the first foyer, holding one hand up to his nose as if to ward off the reek of mold.

'Of course it isn't how you remember it,' Jeff said, and began traversing down one of the aisles to the center stage.

'It's gone to shit, just like everything else here.'

Dillion pointed his flashlight down in order to reveal an aisle's narrow path. With each successive step he took, more of the chapel's features swam into focus. At ground level, further spider webbing was evident, each frothy string like a lattice-work of vines connecting one aisle to another. The smell of the church – like a forgotten cellar only recently opened to the modern age – intensified the closer he came to the lectern.

'Look – the original Bible is still here,' Jeff proclaimed. He'd already reached the pulpit itself, and stood behind the central dais, shining his torch down on the aged parchment of something more akin to a scroll. Inching forward, he blew dust from the surface of its pages. 'Blessed are the dead who die in the Lord from now on,' he read aloud. 'They will rest from their labor, for their deeds will follow them.'

Alyssa had also found her way to the raised pulpit, stepping up to join Dillion at the same well-timed moment. 'Well that's just fitting, isn't it?' she said, shining her torch on the black mop of Jeff's hair. 'It's been flipped open to Revelations all these years. I bet Father Parrington would have an orgasm seeing all of this – his promised apocalypse made flesh.'

'How much do you remember?' Dillion asked her. And (furtively so no one would notice), he casually removed his iPhone.

'All of it,' Alyssa replied flatly. 'Mrs. Cowman was a fan of shuttling us through here every morning after homeroom. Morning prayers and then confession on Tuesdays. I was scared of this place; everyone was.

Thought the holy water by the door would burn right through my hand like acid.'

The crunching sound of footsteps came from their right: Carolina. At the foot of her cheap black boots, a shallow pool of broken plaster lay heaped. She wasn't looking at them, however – Dillion noticed her gaze trained steadily on the rafters above.

'What?' he asked. 'What is it?'

'Holy water didn't frighten me,' she replied. 'That did.'

By a narrow beam of jerky torchlight, Carolina revealed a Christ-impaled crucifix fully seven feet in length. Attached slantwise to one of the upper rafters, the cross was a life-sized caricature intended to brood over the pulpit and visiting audience alike. The Nazarene's face, usually one of mawkish serenity, was instead a brutish countenance seeming to bristle with anger and judgement. Buttressed on a fierce cowlick, a crown of thorns pierced the side of his head in at least a dozen different places, welts that oozed a dripping morass of wine-dark blood. Though Dillion had known about the statue and had anticipated its survival, the sight of it now through their collective beams was enough to genuinely unnerve him. Not for the first time, he pondered the hypocrisy of the Christian faith – a system of belief that inwardly encouraged love yet outwardly projected the macabre.

Dillion said, 'Father Parrington was the chaplain while you were a student?'

'Yes, he was.'

It was Jason who answered the question, the man shuffling slowly down the center aisle like a ghost. Though his features were hard to discern, the suit he wore was not. Headless, it floated up through the murk as though it were a suit alone. *That's Jason's cue to unload,* Dillion thought morbidly. *Time for the man to give us one last confession.* Thumbing the record button, Dillion once more brought out his iPhone in full view of the others. Nobody objected when he took a lingering shot of each of them in turn before finally settling the camera on Jason. He stared back into the phone blearily, as if already exhausted by the night's excursion.

'Mr. Parrington was originally like a father to me, to all of us here in the church.' For a brief moment he seemed to become acutely aware of Christ's visage staring down at them. 'There were five of us back in 1989 – five altar boys under Father Parrington's tutelage. I volunteered here whenever I could, anything was better than being at home with Ma. The school was sometimes strict, but after my dad died …' Jason shook his head sadly. 'Let's just say being at home wasn't a nice place for me to be.'

Dillion, already aware of this part of the tale, had made it apparent to Jason (and everyone else standing beside him), the *crux* of their stories would have to be divulged while filming within the school itself. Specifically, the very locale where things of a supernatural bent had transpired. While such a novel directing technique might be considered cruel for the storyteller, there was no other way to achieve what those in the business lovingly coined *production value*. This, and more, had been outlined in each individual contract. A contract all of them had willingly signed.

'It seems so creepy these days, doesn't it? Little boys

running around and performing errands for old men who believed they were appointed by God? You have to understand, this was at the tail end of the eighties. Most of the high profile cases involving abuse had yet to come to light or were ongoing back then. It was –'

'The same-old lame excuses,' Alyssa interrupted. 'It was a different era, everybody behaved *differently* back then.'

Dillion said, 'Alyssa, *please.*'

'It *was* a different era,' Jason told her. 'And we did do things differently back then. There was … innocence to our faith and duties. Nobody could have predicted what would happen to Father Parrington.'

Alyssa cackled. 'You mean nobody could predict a celibate old man would lose his mind and go bat-shit crazy?'

Ignoring the gibe, Jason merely continued to stare into Dillion's camera with a fixed attention. A mop of fringe, so blonde it sometimes appeared white, plastered his forehead in sweaty curls. After a while Dillion gave him a reassuring nod, his silent cue to proceed.

'As head acolyte I did it all – acted as thurifer and carried the incense, poured wine during consecration, and rang the bell when I was called upon to do so. I participated in communion and sang in the choir. I even cleaned the rectory toilets on occasion. And for most of my tenure, Father Parrington conducted himself in the proper manner befitting a priest. But then one day during the term of lent …'

'Ablutions,' Jeff said from his position at the pulpit.

Jason was nodding vigorously, as if the word and

practice were common knowledge. 'Usually the act entails rinsing the hands first in wine and then in water. But sometimes it means washing parts of the body, typically the feet.'

Dillion thrust his camera back to the pulpit and gave Jeff a beseeching look, hoping the man could read his features in the waning light.

'Word gets around in any school, Mr. Dillion,' the old man said. 'First it travels through the teachers' lounge, and then sometimes it makes its way back to us. Teachers often get talkative with the help after hours.'

Tells of embarrassment had begun to show on Jason's face. 'Father Parrington … at first he requested some of the altar boys wash his feet before mass. I thought it was a little strange, of course, but my mother told me to press on with my duties, just said our Father was a traditional man; a conservative throwback to the old ways. Soon, he had us washing each other's feet, the kind of routine that got some of the older boys talking during recess. And he'd watch us while we did it, too … beaming at us from his couch and stroking his beard.'

'Jesus wept,' Alyssa muttered.

'He had his favorite helpers for tasks, myself and another boy named Gifford. Working in tandem he made us wash his feet … and it wasn't long before he requested other parts of his body, too.'

Swallowing hard, Dillion cleared his throat to make it heard above a whisper. 'Would you say all of this was going on around the same time Father Parrington's sermons were becoming … more erratic within the school?'

Jason nodded, even more eagerly than before. 'Not just

during school mass, either. But on Sundays when a lot of our parents were present. Long sermons about Christ's eventual return. Nothing overly strange there, but his message soon became more irrational, how the school *itself* could well be ground zero for the second coming, and how we would need to set up the proper infrastructure for his return. And then … then Father Parrington began to hear voices.'

'Voices?' Dillion asked. 'What do you mean voices?'

Slowly, Jason raised his eyes to the ceiling. Again, their collective light found the Nazarene's face, and Carolina released a small hiccup of fright.

'He began talking to the statue, too. Even during his spiels. Snatching quick looks up at the ceiling and muttering under his breath. It was like … like he was receiving instructions from it or something.'

Revealed in the crossbeams: bloody hands and bloody feet pinioned in penance. Also transparent to a degree: a niggling impression the statue had inched closer to them with Jason's revelations. Up until this very moment, Dillion had felt relatively calm concerning tonight's adventure. But now he could feel the first faint stirrings of … what? Genuine unease? Fear? Was such a thing possible this late in the game? Over the past decade, he had wandered many unquiet places of the world: barren buildings where fingerprints from the past often seem to linger in the unseen molecules of the air itself. Nonetheless, there had always been a novelty element behind the foreboding – a carnival feeling of exploration, of ghost-train spectacle and childhood escapade.

But not so here. No siree. Providence Place, for all its

pleasing production value, feels rotten to the fucking core.
Christ stared back accusingly, his somber brown eyes like a dark well-spring into another world.

'But it wasn't really the statue talking, was it?' Carolina whispered. 'It was the *school.*'

A simple, almost nonchalant statement – but one seeming to carry a huge amount of import for the former students. In modest terms, Carolina had just summed up what they had all been thinking but hadn't, up until now, given voice to: that behind every freakish occurrence or unexplained event here, something burned behind the scenes like an obscure architect. And, though the priest himself had inadvertently become its spokesperson, there was always another engineer pulling at the controls like a puppeteer.

For the third time in his tale, Jason nodded robustly. He said, 'It's as good an explanation as any. Whatever was eating away at Father Parrington, it soon began to manifest itself in other ways.'

'Other ways?' Alyssa asked.

'On his body. On his flesh.'

Using both thumb and forefinger, Dillion zoomed in even closer to Jason's sweaty face. This was one part of the story he had not anticipated.

'We saw them as we washed his naked body, huge welts on his upper torso like teeth marks. Sometimes they were red, and sometimes they were white and quivering, blister things filled with pus. Only I don't think it was pus at all. This was something else; like something alive was battening onto his body, making it their own.'

Dillion didn't need sufficient light to make out the

horrified expressions Alyssa and Carolina both wore. Jeff, unawares, had crept over to them from his position by the pulpit. Judging from his own wide-eyed stare, it appeared his earlier claim of immunity from the school's malevolence was perhaps duplicitous.

'And you didn't report any of this?' Alyssa asked incredulously. 'Didn't tell your teachers the priest was potentially infected with something?'

'I was frightened. Terrified, really. Around this time I began feeling the church working on me, too.'

Since first pulling up in his Ford, Dillion had not felt an abundance of empathy regarding his human cast. They were grown adults, down on their luck in the real world, and needed fiscal motivation to return to their past. *Just remember*, a colleague had told him when the germ of Providence Place was still a young idea in his mind. *The school itself is your star – a character brimming with endless possibilities. And one that requires no direction or pampering.*

But now … now Dillion was beginning to see something else here: a scarred man who had returned to a haunted room. And so far hadn't cracked under its weight.

'I think you all know the rest of the story,' Jason said. 'Most of it, anyway. One of the teachers branded it the final sermon, a sensationalist title but a fitting one, I think. On Sunday, December 5th of that year, Father Parrington mounted the pulpit and told us Judgement Day was upon us and Christ had finally returned. By this stage he was hardly recognizable, the blisters, growths - whatever they were had sprouted into his neck, arms, and legs. I wasn't even on duty that day, but I came over anyway because I felt somehow compelled to. Because the school … it *wanted me to.*'

In the dark Jason looked at the others in turn, as if sensing or seeking skepticism. Seeing none, he said, 'A curtain was raised halfway up, the back one where everybody entered for confession. By this stage I think most of the audience present would have left … except they didn't. No one did. Somehow, I think they were all transfixed by the same power that had compelled me to come. What the curtain revealed, what was *behind* the curtain, I still dream about to this day. Father Parrington had fashioned his own cross, you see, one he must have spent weeks making – and mounted on this one was a real human being, my best friend Gifford, crucified the night before and his wounds still bleeding afresh.'

Dillion pushed the camera even closer to Jason's face, so that his bulbous head appeared enlarged, almost premature.

'Gifford was very dead, of course. But his eyes were still open. And he stared down at the church audience with blood dripping from his own crown of thorns. There were gasps, shrieks, but most of the din came from Father Parrington himself – in an ecstasy of prayer and supplication. He'd made this sacrifice, you see; to bring about his foretold revelations. And now he was waiting for the trumpets to begin their blaring.'

For Dillion, it was all too easy to imagine this scenario; because he'd read the account for the first time over two years ago: Father Parrington relieving himself of his vestments, falling to his knees, and then proceeding to violently rake his sores and lesions, beseeching the room with shaking hands. And, like one of the plagues visited upon the citizens of Egypt, his body had fallen into absolute decay. By the time the waling priest had staggered to the first pew, the man was already dead ... a victim of his own maladies and madness.

There were many more subtleties to the story, of course, but Jason had fallen completely silent. Now came the part where each member of the party became acutely aware of the surroundings: that a young boy had been flayed and exposed no more than seven feet from their current position. Added to this: Father Parrington's final resting place was, in all actuality, located at their very feet.

Sobering, nullifying, the moment seemed like the perfect cue for the church to finally make its presence known to the hapless trespassers.

In earnest, the screaming began.

And didn't stop for some time.

It was something anticipated ... something Dillion *desired* above all else for his picture. A manifestation. A tangible and concrete exhibition that went beyond the Hollywood tripe. Now that it was here, he felt his insides loosen and his balls retract. Unconsciously, he had huddled closer to Jason – as if the child within him were seeking some kind of maternal succor.

Screaming ... unbroken and full of agony. The kind of piercing wail one might expect if torture had been recorded and documented for posterity or pleasure. Sometimes it was close to them; hovering in and around the wall closet to the pulpit, then taking a diving turn and traversing the ceiling before skating along the floor and finding the walls again. In Dillion's initial surprise, he'd accidentally pointed the camera toward his shirt, no doubt muffling the audio quality substantially. With the shock wearing off, he righted his iPhone, trying to follow the sound as it wove around the room like something damned seeking release.

Only Alyssa seemed unaffected. Though their flashlights were pointed toward the concrete below, Dillion could make out her features following the sound as though she were intently curious. She whispered, 'Is it a woman? Or a man? God, it sounds more like an animal.'

'It sounds like nothing I've ever heard before,' said Carolina. She had also huddled closer to Jason – probably for the same reason as Dillion.

Jeff had retreated again, making slow steps along the circumference of the wall as if trying to track its source. In another circumstance, Dillion might have laughed; the small shadow of the man appeared vaguely cartoonish, almost like a khaki-clad jungle explorer. He would stop, listen with his head cocked, and then move off swiftly again in a striding gait.

Then, as abruptly as the scream had started, it ceased – cut off somewhere above them in the attic fixtures. Jeff appeared crestfallen, his elusive hunt over for now.

Shining his torch directly into the man's chest, Dillion asked, 'I don't suppose you ever heard anything like *that* while you were working here? Never once?'

Still keeping his eyes trained on the ceiling, Jeff merely shook his head slowly.

'Play it back,' said Alyssa, a note of excitement in her voice. 'Play it back, and let's hear it again.'

Carolina looked on the verge of snatching the camera out of Dillion's grasp. 'No,' she said, emphatically. 'God no. Please don't.'

'What are you afraid of?' Alyssa asked her.

'Someone's clearly fucking with us. Probably our director, here. Did you honestly think things would heat up this early in the hunt?'

From the tone of her voice, Carolina appeared offended. 'And you *didn't*? What do you think we're playing with, Alyssa? Harmless matchsticks? I saw the way you were looking at the school when I hopped in the car. You can drop the tough-girl act right now, because it won't win you any friends here.'

A significant portion of Dillion's beam illuminated Alyssa's face enough for him to discern her shock. With little doubt, there had been a social pecking order while these two were students of Providence Place. And Alyssa's hierarchy in the scheme of things had clearly been well above the fat woman standing next to her. Perhaps she'd assumed that order would still stand today; even now … here in this derelict world where children were crucified, and where priests were stigmatized with pus symptomatic to those possessed.

'Nobody's fucking with us,' Jeff said from the shadows. Though the two women continued to stare at each other, the ex-cleaner's lucid tone had thankfully quelled the moment. 'This is it, ladies and gentleman. The unseen world we came here to see. And something tells me shit's only going to get worse from here on out.'

There it was: an admission their journey would continue. Continue, despite the evidence something malign had now marked their presence in Providence Place.

The show would go on.

For a moment, Dillion's emotions flailed – because a part of him (that childish, monster-in-the-closet part), had assumed the group might potentially hightail it back to the waiting cars outside. He had evidence in his hands; *good* evidence. And, like so many over-eager millennials living in the world today, he suddenly felt an irresistible urge to upload it somewhere as quickly as possible … if only to ascertain its existence.

But then his rational mind kicked in; his *director's* mind.

'Jeff,' he said. 'There's a small cleaning room not far from here, over by the prep school. Did you want to check it out before we go any further?'

Pointing the camera away from Jason, Dillion observed the hand that held it was shaking. Not timidly, either. By the time Jeff had moved within its radius of light, he had somehow managed to suppress the worst of it.

'No, Mr. Dillion. That's a *very* small broom closet. One we rarely used, if ever. I believe I'll tell *my* story when we reach the main cleaners' room, which is a hop, skip and a jump from the library.'

Jeff's story, he thought to himself. Dear God, this really *was* just the beginning.

Bringing his voice up an octave, he tried to inject what he hoped was something approaching humor into his next words. 'Which is the next port-of-call, ladies and gentleman. Although there's no librarians in tow with us tonight, that doesn't mean it escapes our inventory. C'mon, let's get out of here.'

Taking the lead as he did walking into the chapel, Dillion made his way past the many pews, then up the narrow incline of a dark aisle, and finally back out into a world where the air felt more or less breathable … and where the threat of screams and a past trying to intrude was not something all-encompassing.

FOUR

A one word mantra kept a steady pace in Alyssa's head, one that (although not pleasant), at least kept her grounded and held the fear at bay.

Bitch.

Knowing Carolina did not deserve the title did little to dissuade her misgivings, however. The woman had embarrassed her. In front of others, no less. She'd been stood down by a girl whose overriding walrus physique had been the punchline of many jokes initiated by Alyssa herself.

Bitch.

The adult side of her told her to shut the hell up; the teenager within gawped at the injustice of it all. Although walking up to her smug, freckled face and slapping it would feel wholly satisfying, for now the more mature side of her psyche held things in check.

For now.

Alyssa lit up her second smoke in as many minutes.

At least ten minutes had passed since their exit from the chapel. Currently, all five members of the night's expedition were navigating a three-tiered stairway that would eventually bring them to the school's massive library. At the very front, Dillion and Jeff were talking amiably in muted tones among themselves. Immediately behind them, Jason Wedle traversed each riser slowly, his left hand skating the filthy bannister. And following closely behind *him*, the walrus, her white silhouette like the cardboard cut-out of a fat ghost.

Ghost.

A common word; a common noun used so often in everyday life its very meaning seemed to have lost its original purpose and flavor. Not here, though … not in a place where the stairs were encrusted with dirt and fungus; where deflated, blackened basketballs sat perched on the risers like obscene signposts lighting the way for them. And chances were they had already heard one: a caterwauling like the churning stomach of the school itself. Of course, she had attributed that elegy to some form of shenanigans; to Dillion Cook placing it and perhaps similar traps along every stage of their route to ultimately give his film much-needed verisimilitude. But deep in her heart she knew better. Because of the theater; because of what she'd seen in the dressing rooms when –

But I won't think about that now. Not yet.

Soon the others had scaled the top, and Alyssa mounted the final stair shortly thereafter. Here the balcony was even more haphazard than below, if such a thing were possible: the grey outlines of ancient tables and bookcases pulled from inside the building and piled atop one another like a child's building blocks. And always seeming to cover every inch of matter: a smutty layer of dust like a supernatural glaze. The entrance to the library itself (two conjoined doors composed of wire mesh and glass) had long since been removed from their hinges and lay scattered in pieces.

Where they had once stood: a gaping black hole led into an unknown darkness.

Gathering in a slack knot near the entrance, the group's torch discharges made cross-beams of shadow like a wake of searchlights. Observing Dillion as he filmed the environs and made his dramatic annotations, Alyssa struggled not to make another witticism at his expense. This was a facet of her everyday personality she usually embraced and seldom apologized for (having a cynical mouth often worked to a person's advantage in the real world), but wise cracking now would only make her appear more foolish and vulnerable in front of the others. Something Carolina had accomplished with relative ease.

'The library is shaped like a rectangular archway,' Dillion told them after completing his commentary. 'But you don't need me to tell you that. We'll follow it through and simply come out the other side. It'll be *very* dark, so let's all stick close together. And if any of you have any stories, things you remember from the time you spent here, don't hesitate to spill them.'

A wordless exchange of glances flitted through the group. *Did* anyone remember anything outwardly sinister taking place within the library? From the uncertain looks of all present, it seemed nobody had … although this didn't stop the coil of unease Alyssa felt about stepping in there.

She remembered the wide circumference of the library hallway being somewhat huge. Once they were in, there were no quick or easy exits to be had.

Without further comment, Dillion turned around and walked through the door-less maw serving as the library's entrance. In his wake (and wanting to present some kind of brave fortitude), Alyssa stepped ahead of the others to quickly follow.

A pithy show of strength, but in a pecking order still largely undecided, she had to begin somewhere.

First grey shadow, then absolute darkness. Like stepping from one world and into another. No more than ten steps taken into the hallway and already the suffocating weight of the building and pitch-black darkness seemed overly oppressive. The chapel had smelled bad; this smelled even worse – a prickly miasma of cold storage places and rotting marine life. With Dillion's footfalls acting as a compass, Alyssa proceeded hesitantly, the beam from her flashlight revealing nothing but scorched green linoleum on the ground below.

It doesn't matter that nobody remembers anything about the library, she thought now, staring down at her sneakers with a dull intensity. *Perhaps evil didn't always reign here, but it sure as shit has a permanent home now.*

Ahead, Dillion's footfalls abruptly ceased. No doubt he stood before the first classroom … which (Alyssa vaguely remembered) was the children's portion of the library. There were at least half-a-dozen different rooms running the length of the arched hallway, each one of them having served a different purpose relative to different grade levels: two computer rooms; a drama room for school plays; further down another room for high-school fiction and a separate one for text books. Alyssa also recalled floors cushioned by beanbags and even the odd television monitor and gaming console ...

None of that was apparent now as the dark outline of their director moved forward, his twin light assault – one of camera and one of torch – revealing walls caked in grime and garlanded with graffiti. No children's scribblings, either. No, this was the artistry of squatters and miscreants. A side wall on their left (no doubt once home to book posters) was now a repository for various kinds of etched depravity ... lewd words and even lewder representations of crude acts performed by the naked human anatomy. There were cocks spurting juice and entering holes; cocks being stroked and manhandled by horned things with tails and teeth. An abundance of different-sized breasts fought for attention with long-legged women performing cunnilingus on each other. Buttocks, vaginas, and even bestiality – seemingly no part of the room had escaped the onslaught.

'*Disgusting,*' Carolina muttered from behind. Like Jason before her in the chapel, she spoke around a finger-pinched nose. The library's reek (like stale piss and other fluids), could almost be read like dust-particles through their flashlights' beams. 'I don't suppose any of you thought to bring a weapon of some kind? Dillion ...'

But Carolina got no further. Rooted to the spot, she stared at the center of the room with avid wonder. Alyssa stared, too. So did Jeff and Jason, both of whom were huddled against the door. Dillion (perhaps with Carolina's question beating a rhythmic tattoo through his head) tiptoed lightly toward their next find, his iPhone trained in a specialized slant as though he were framing the shot with his fingers.

Many chairs, unquestionably man-made circles of them, radiated out from the room's heart like a drawn pictograph. And sitting on the chairs were different-sized mannequins and dolls. While some were child-sized (Alyssa recognized a uniformed papier-mâché creation pilfered directly from the foyer of the admin building), others were fully dressed adults fresh from a showroom floor. The closest was a male mannequin sporting a bowler hat, black business attire, and a face smeared with so much white greasepaint his countenance appeared grotesque in the wan light.

Grinning at the group, he seemed to be saving the core enthusiasm of his smile for Alyssa only.

Next to him, a pudgy girl wearing nothing but a see-through bodice canted her head severely toward the middle of the circle … toward the *real* human being who stood within the ring of chairs as though extolling lessons to its audience of mannequins.

No way. Ah-ah. Can't be real. For one thing, it looks like a fucking scarecrow.

Then why was it moving?

Propelled by fascination more than anything else, Alyssa moved closer, shining her torch directly on the apparition and trying to get a foothold on its particulars. Like many of the other mannequins, it bore some kind of strange hat, the front of which obscured a flat face devoid of features. Its movements, languid and furtive, were centered on its arms. Suddenly, fight or flight seemed a real possibility, and Alyssa was about to succumb to one of them when Dillion shouted something incoherent.

Then, in a quieter tone just above a whisper, 'I think it's just ... more rodents.'

As if in response the scarecrow shape twisted abruptly, its misshapen anatomy coming apart in an orgy of flying forms. Within the melee, Alyssa bore witness to beady eyes and thrusting whiskers; she glimpsed a gross accumulation of moving body parts that dived, scattered, and finally fell to the floor in a hot rain of jostling limbs and fur.

Mice! Her mind screamed in numb, dumb wonder. *It's a goddamn infestation – the kind of plague one would see on a farm.*

Freaked by the collective light, hundreds of mice swarmed out of the body of the mannequin like coordinated birds in flight. No longer supported by their multitude, the scarecrow form began to unravel, its checkered shirt and denim trousers caving in a timely precision. And as the exterior dissolved, so too did its inner framework – a seething archipelago of fiberglass, plastic, and mouse droppings.

Just wait for it, she thought. *Any second now –*

Carolina, her voice bouncing off the walls and amplified by the lack of objects, screamed. Knocking a mannequin off its perch, she straddled a chair and proceeded to climb it, barely avoiding the horde as it dove forward around the legs of the chair. Some, enraptured by the movement, scuttled *up* the chair, covering every niche as though the ground itself were moving. Which it appeared to be doing.

'Enough of this shit,' she heard Dillion say. Apparently satisfied with his existing footage, he'd pocketed his iPhone. 'Everyone – get to the next room.' Needing no persuasion, Alyssa backtracked. Jeff and Jason did the same. Carolina remained anchored to her seat, gripping the headrest and staring down at the floor as though she were adrift on a sea of lava. Building into a sprint, Alyssa felt a hollow *crunch* as one of the rodents beneath her sneakers succumbed to its weight. Then another. And yet one more. By the time she'd reached the exit, at least a dozen of them had perished beneath her soles.

Even more little deaths added to a place that stank of it.

Completely bereft of chairs and mannequins (wholly lacking anything substantial beside a singular fan), the next classroom *did* contain a working lightbulb. Enough for the group to make out no graffiti or obscene images decorated the walls. The same effect Alyssa had experienced stepping into the library (traversing worlds), was here applied again. Though its effect was even more startling. For reasons unknown, the architect – or *architects* – of the mannequin circle had found the children's library vastly more appealing for their debauchery. As if the lingering residue of innocence there had caused them to call it home.

'What do we do now?' said Jason. Up until this moment the man had appeared stoic, almost indifferent to the atmosphere pervading the library. Now he paced, pulling anxiously at the bottom of his tie. 'There are *people* here, in the school. Bums and degenerates probably. Did you see all that hoodoo on the walls? Like something from another century. And the dolls? What was that? They're hiding, in the building. Waiting. And now they know we are, too. They'll come –'

'Quiet,' the walrus said. She'd been the last to arrive, reaching the next classroom a full three minutes after the others had made their exit. Though it had taken Carolina some time and courage to step off her chair, her initial revulsion and response to the plague had apparently vanished. 'We *don't* know anyone else is here in the building with us. Whoever made that room is probably long gone by now.'

Jeff had found the floor, his back leaning against a bare wall; his forearms placed on his knees. Pointing a finger at Carolina, he said, 'Yes! The mice confirm that, don't they? They've been allowed to breed in the school for God knows how long because there's nobody else around to disturb them. And there's dust everywhere, we all saw it.'

Outside in the hallway, the steady click of paws had receded. Retreating also was the powerful smell, having been replaced by a more mundane species of decay.

Dillion said, 'Turn off your beams. We don't need them in here.'

Alyssa obliged, frowning. She looked down at Jeff. 'Why are you so keen to stay all of a sudden? That room might be long abandoned, but it's obvious others could still be hanging around.'

'That's not what he meant,' Carolina said. 'He just means we're safe here for the time being. Isn't that right?'

In reply, Jeff nodded slowly.

Jason had stopped his pacing, and now stood staring at the western wall as if the mannequins on the other side were only seconds away from breaking through. 'I just don't know. Things suddenly feel *wrong*. Tell me you all don't feel it, too? That scarecrow teacher thing, what was it for? And the mice, where's the source of their food coming from?'

'Teenagers,' Alyssa said flatly. 'Bored teenagers dressing up big dollies and spray-painting the walls with filth. Probably making a death metal film-clip for all we know. Christ knows it's the perfect place for it.'

But Jason wasn't convinced. Taking his eyes off the wall, he sauntered up to Alyssa and peered at her indignantly. 'Perhaps you should go back in there, then, rummage around a little more and find out?'

Alyssa could only stare at him.

'Didn't think so,' Jason said. He was shaking his head. 'Anyone else here volunteering to go back in and have a look-see?'

'No one's going back in,' Dillion said. 'I've got what I need. Carolina, what's in the next room?'

Standing frozen and hypnotized by the hallway, Carolina snapped back into the present. She looked at Dillion tiredly. 'Computers, if I remember correctly.'

Camera rolling again, Dillion trained its small screen over the white walls and pockmarked carpet. For a moment, he lingered on the room's solitary light source: a naked bulb whose dirty inner casing was encrusted with moths.

'Then let's go. We still have a ton of ground to cover.'

*

A return to the hallway, and a return to absolute darkness. Though beveled windows grazed the entire northern flank of the building, Alyssa could discern nothing through their glass except the purple gauze of full night. Walking beside Dillion this time, she could feel the presage of the children's library behind them like a living vice, beckoning her to look around ... to glance back just once and make sure nothing was following them. But she resisted the impulse. When you deprived the dark of your attention, it gave you none in return. At least, a part of her insisted this was so.

Bullshit. That's just a childhood fancy and you know it. Whatever force was in there, it's only letting you go now because it wants to meet you up close and personal later. When your little group arrives at the theater, for instance. A girl holding a noose is calling you home ...

Alyssa suddenly felt her body give way to a shudder which almost sent her sprawling. Though she had managed to avoid (thus far) unreserved panic, the sensation itself hovered over the outer fringes of her awareness.

'Alyssa? Are you okay up there?'

It was Jason's voice, an anchor keeping her temporarily grounded. Somehow, he'd perceived her discomfort.

'Just dandy,' she shot back. 'Look, we're here already.'

Footsteps echoed along the hallway, five separate pairs of shoes coming to rest before yet another darkened doorway. Adjacent to them sat a broad column of evenly spaced lockers – wooden cubes whose numbers formed an intricate gridding. Dillion, infusing them with the light of his camera, revealed portions that still contained objects inside: there were hessian school bags and used cans of tuna. Broken crayons and pencil cases fought for space alongside dirty, blue baseball caps. On the lower ends, Alyssa spied sticky-taped nametags bearing the scrawl of children who would, in all probability, have children of their own by now.

'Creepy,' Dillion muttered. Predictably, his camera loitered on the individual names, giving an audience to objects that had sat in darkness now for over a decade.

Jeff said, 'It's like a shipwreck. That's what I keep thinking of. Like any second now a slow-moving fish is going to move through one of our beams.'

'Did you catch that, Dillion?' With thoughts of the theater passing, Alyssa could feel a modicum of her old self (and something akin to calm) returning. 'I think you should hand over narration duties to Jeff here. What do you say, Jeff? Think you can keep up that kind of shtick?'

Ignoring the gibe completely, Dillion moved his camera away from the lockers and shone it into the first stages of the computer room. With the contents inside slowly revealed, Jeff's metaphor of a shipwreck gained sudden, shocking weight. The computers, all of which were archaic models of a bygone era, were caked in so much grime they appeared coarse with it. At least a dozen in all, their flat grey cathode screens stared at the newcomers like portals into some strange nowhere.

About to proceed in, Alyssa caught Dillion by the arm. 'We don't have to go in there, do we? I mean … look. It's all here right in front of us. I say we make for the library's exit as quickly as possible. Just get on with things, you know?'

Their guide frowned, seeming to weigh the pros and cons of her statement as if deciphering the words of a child. Seemingly on the verge of protest, Dillion abruptly succumbed and sagged in relief.

'Perhaps you're right,' he said. 'We came here for the film. There might be a story in the library, but it's not one pertinent to my players.'

Another rejoinder was forming on Alyssa's lips, this one begging release. *Players.* The word smacked of a kind of bleak deceptiveness on their director's part. Was this all they were to him? Actors on a stage to be paraded around? Never mind the story of Providence Place was a very real one, and the gathered motley crew here were very real people. Feeding the thought, Alyssa was suddenly bombarded with an avid recollection of every director and producer she had ever worked with: from those who wanted nothing more than to see her tits on camera; to that even viler breed who desired to see her writhing on a dressing room floor for favors bestowed. They were all alike, it seemed. Vultures who preyed on the unsuspecting for personal gain.

As if echoing her sentiments, Carolina said, 'We're not actors, Dillion. And this isn't a damn set.'

Embarrassed, Dillion brandished his camera at them. 'I *know* that. And it's not what I meant. It's your *stories* that are important here, of course. If we don't get a move on something could happen before they're told.'

This seemed to be the spur to get walking once again,

Alyssa now taking up the vanguard. With each successive classroom drifting into view, the group continued on, navigating a linoleum floor strewn with waterlogged books swollen to the size of dictionaries. Moments later the end of the corridor came into focus.

Quickening her pace at the sight of it, Alyssa was halted once more when Dillion called out from behind.

'Wait,' he said to them. 'I need a few shots of the fiction section first.'

Now close enough to reach out and touch the exit, Alyssa could only frown at the doorway. Although nothing was visible on the other side, there was an obvious change of color through the steel-mesh window: a reddish opaque light signaling freedom on the other side.

Turning around, she saw Dillion had already disappeared.

Again they were in luck: when Dillon flicked the wall switch this time, five separate banks of lights slowly phased into existence. Having been neglected for so long, it was as if the bulbs here were tricked into doing their own handiwork. Perhaps (somewhat expectedly) one of the banks remained stuttering, its caustic wattage giving off a jaundiced strobe effect.

Suddenly feels as if we're in a fucking video game, Alyssa thought, following Dillion into the library with unhurried steps. Inside, Jeff stood rooted to the spot, staring at the walls once again with his own special brand of dumb wonder. Jason, hands stuffed deeply within the pocket-creases of his overcoat, was eyeing an ancient and yellowed registration desk.

'Oh, shit. Look at this.'

Though Dillion's voice was soft, the silence of the library augmented it. Positioned in the center aisle, he was treading softly amidst a small flotilla of reading desks. To his left and right, various shelves containing a moldering array of paperback books were lined up in serried ranks. Whatever had claimed his attention lay embedded in the floor.

Walking over, Alyssa saw it before she could ask the question: a snail's trail of brown spillage like chocolate milk. Except this wasn't chocolate milk, of course. Browned and mottled with age, an unmistakable emission of blood led a path toward the family of reading desks. It was here (the spot Dillion now occupied), where whatever had produced the trail had come to its final resting place, the slick lines coagulating into one fecund mass.

Whatever died here, died violently.

'Could've been an animal,' Jason ventured. 'You know … a sacrifice or something.'

No one replied. Dillion (bearing an uncanny resemblance to forensics) traced his camera over the width of the killing floor, muttering unintelligible narration in the process. Only now did Alyssa notice other matter was collected in the center maelstrom: an assortment of bones and their inner marrow.

'This,' said Jeff, 'is no sacrifice. I have a friend who has spent a lifetime working in crime-scene cleaning. And this … this looks like something, or *someone*, was dragged through here kicking and screaming. And then tortured and murdered at the end of it all.'

'And you know this because of secondhand accounts from a friend?' Carolina asked.

Jeff shook his head. 'Just look at it closely and tell me what you see?'

But Alyssa wanted to look no longer. Because it was all too easy to envisage Jeff's scenario. Beginning at the registration desk, a human being had been collared, possibly stabbed. Then (screaming and clawing at their assailant), the individual had been lugged through the center aisle of the library, trailing their innards and life-stuff behind them. Pulled by something or someone far more powerful than itself ... then finally butchered on the carpet, the killer not resting until the meat was fully dismembered.

'Well, then,' said Jason. 'Where's the body now?'

Jeff's riposte was cat-quick and full of scorn. 'How the hell should I know? It could be one of those mannequins in the children's library for all we know.'

Now *that* was a thought Alyssa wouldn't contemplate. Shaking subtly, she reached into her jeans and pulled out her Lucky Strikes. Though Dillion shot her a disapproving glance she dutifully ignored the film-maker, holding a cigarette up to her face and lighting it with a jittering flame. She said, 'Let's just get the fuck out of here, what do you say?'

'Hang on,' Dillion said. 'I need to see if there's anything else in here.'

'Like what?'

Without a reply he turned his back to them and began investigating the bookshelves. When he was finished with them he scrutinized the corners, cupboards, and lastly the registration desk, ruffling through its many drawers like a scavenger. Finally, wearing a look of wan disappointment, he said, 'Everything's empty. Jeff, I believe it's time for you to escort us to the cleaning rooms.'

An inscrutable smile – either of contempt or smug satisfaction – surfaced on Jeff's features. For a while he merely regarded the group, as if privy to a wealth of secrets they could only guess at.

'I'll lead the way,' he said.

FIVE

Jeff Wolfe recalled many things about Providence Place – but one thing in particular that lingered (clinging to his consciousness like the stuff it was composed of) was how much goddamn chewing gum he'd had to peel off on a daily basis. The little brats had known how much Jeff despised the sticky stuff. So of course they had gone out of their way to make sure copious amounts of both varieties (bubble and chewing) were spread out under their desks, on their lockers, and occasionally ground into the carpet. Sometimes he'd spend over an hour removing one piece with detergent, often staying past his allocated hours until the streetlights outside were the only source of light pervading the courtyards. To this day he still dreamed about everything his job here had entailed: vacuuming, mopping, and wiping shit off the restroom tiles. On some nights he dreamed of chewing gum so thick and viscous it blanketed the entire school in a pink and white halo of synthetic rubber.

He'd recalled the chewing gum, yes – but he recalled the unseen world even more.

On Jeff's very first week as site manager, the unseen world around Providence Place had made itself known by murdering one of his workers, young Matthew Thrane. Matthew had been twenty-four years old and studying at a local university. Employed as a cleaner part-time, Matthew had committed suicide in one of the cleaner's closets by pouring undiluted bleach down his throat, slicing an artery in his left arm with a paint scraper, and finally tying a trash bag around his head to induce asphyxiation before the bleach could properly do its work.

Suicide had been on the death certificate.

But Matthew Thrane had not committed suicide.

The unseen world had induced the poor boy.

Coming across the body at the end of his shift, Jeff had known this immediately. Although barely glimpsing so much as a shadow up until that moment, the sight of Matthew's lifeless corpse was all the evidence he had needed. Of course, the malignancy could be felt when one merely stepped into the building, a darkness that could produce restrained nausea, but Matthew's bulging eyes and contorted features were the final piece of the puzzle. The kid had died terrified. The kid had died against his will.

Providence Place was alive, yet its unseen world desired all living things to suffer.

In the aftermath of the tragedy, any sane man would have pulled up stakes then and there and made off for better employment. But Jeff would not be cowed so easily. Though the school was undoubtedly haunted, he would continue to do his work; he would face the beast head on and deal with it accordingly. Besides, it wasn't the worst place he had ever cleaned up shit, if one could believe that.

For the next two years, nothing much of import happened in Providence Place. Nothing with supernatural overtures, anyway.

Not until the day Marcy Ribald joined his cleaning team.

Blighted shadows and full night made the steps descending from the library harder to navigate, and each of them made use of the bannisters to avoid tripping as they made their way down to a small courtyard. With night the temperature had (predictably) plummeted, and Jeff offered up silent thanks he had chosen to don his old-school trench coat before leaving his one-room apartment in Alpine Estates. Insulated, the coat also contained an abundance of pockets in which to conceal things … like a pistol, for instance. The others might be scared – which was certainly healthy – but Jeff knew the school more intimately than any of them. He knew the dangers here could be maimed, and he also knew they sometimes carried a human face.

'Watch the last step,' Dillion called out. 'There's some kind of crap on it.'

Alyssa, reaching the final step now, inspected her toes. 'Ectoplasm?'

'I don't think so,' he replied, and barked out a forlorn little laugh. 'Looks more like spilled yogurt.'

'Icky,' Carolina remarked. 'Must be a thousand years old.'

Arriving at the bottom Jeff could ascertain yogurt was

indeed the splashed element. In addition to chewing gum, yogurt had been a popular food item the kids had loved to fling around. Or simply pour into a trashcan from its container, dribbling the gruel down the sides so the cleaners would cop the brunt of it on their clothes when they emptied the trash later that night. More often than not, the garbage bags would simply break from the weight of so much discarded food, flooding the cans themselves with biscuits, sandwiches, and half-eaten apples crawling with flies. Although maintenance workers during the day were supposed to take care of such accidents, they almost never did, and the shit-scrubbers were the ones to ultimately pay the price in stained clothing and reeking hands.

Multiple torch beams revealed the mess so Jeff and Jason could side-step it as they completed the stairway. 'All good, Jeff?' Dillion asked. 'You look like you swallowed something nasty.'

'I'm just recalling how foul my job sometimes was, Mr. Dillion. Truth be told, retirement was the best thing to ever happen to me.'

'I'll bet.'

Jeff purveyed the courtyard, a small niche containing two sets of high-school lockers and some wall shrubbery more commonly known as 'climbers' to anyone in the know. Left unkempt, the creeping plants now covered every available inch of space, green tendrils extending their reach like a hive of fleshy coral. Peering closely at the lockers, Jeff could make out a procession of fat ants trundling toward some unknown bonanza of food. Also noticing them, Alyssa sidled up to the small army, running her torch along the convoy. Meandering in a seemingly innocuous line, the ants' destination ended abruptly in a locker at ground level. Here, they made use of a thin gap at the bottom, entering and exiting the fissure with the hurried dexterity of passengers in a terminal. Bending over, Alyssa reached down with one hand and tentatively placed it on the handle.

'Don't,' Jason warned her.

Appearing almost ready to launch a tackle, Carolina said, 'I wouldn't.'

'Alyssa, wait,' Dillion said. Moving in closer, he alighted his camera on the locker and framed the shot. 'Okay, go.'

Once sporting a combination lock, the small closet had succumbed to the years and weathering, making it obsolete. With scarcely a jerk from Alyssa's hand, the door swung wide, producing a rustic chime. As it did so a small panoply of blowflies were jettisoned out. Alyssa recoiled; Carolina made a gagging sound in the back of her throat.

'Stand back,' Dillion ordered them, and began filming the contents.

Canted to one side, the severed head ended abruptly in a rough patchwork of gore and splayed tendons. Its left side – currently black with ants – had been chiseled away to reveal the bone beneath. Though some fur remained on its skull (sticking up in small islands), the portion left had simply been expunged.

Jason asked, 'Is it a dog?'

'I think so,' Dillion replied. He held the camera out at arm's length, simultaneously pushing it closer and stepping back at the same time. 'Though it could easily be a cat as well.'

'Ah, *now* I can smell it,' Alyssa said. 'Gross.'

'This could be what was killed in the library,' Jason said.

Wishful thinking, Jeff thought. *We all know that wasn't a goddamn animal.*

But no one said anything as they studied the creature, a tacit fascination creeping in. Although observing ants d evour anything was unwholesome, there was an unmistakable allure here akin to watching someone pop a pimple. They crawled through the nose cavity and mouth; they scuttled through the ear canal. A small contingent lingered on what remained of one decaying eye.

'All right, enough of this shit,' Dillion said, and snapped off his iPhone. 'Jeff, point the way to the cleaning closet.'

Obliging, Jeff took the lead. Through the courtyard they walked, then past four rows of drinking fountains whose sinks and troughs were green with calcium, leaves, and lime deposits. More rubbish was piled in massive drifts along the walkway, everything from stale mattresses to more sporting equipment. Further down Jeff spotted a crate of wine, full bottles stamped with the emblem of Providence Place.

'They made wine here?' Carolina asked. 'I don't remember that.'

'Was after your time,' Jeff replied. 'But, yes, the students sometimes made wine in the science building. Parents ended up causing a stink, of course, saying it promoted binge drinking amongst the youth. And they were probably right, too. The line ended up being discontinued. Surprised there's still some of it around.'

Jason made a beeline for the crate and pulled out a bottle, holding the label up to his light. 'We used this wine during mass,' he said. 'Gosh, I'd almost forgotten about it. The faculty also drank it in the teachers' lounge after parent-teacher nights.'

Carolina had joined him. 'That reminds me. Dillion, why did you only seek out students and a cleaner for your film? Why not the teachers who worked here as well? Surely they have just as much to say as any of us.'

Now filming the crate, Dillion said, 'I tried. There are no more retired teachers living in the greater Cranston area.'

'None?'

'None that I could find. Jason, hand me that bottle. I might like me a souvenir.'

Somewhat reluctantly, Jason handed the bottle over.

He was contemplating breaking the seal and taking a sip, Jeff thought. *I'll be damned if he wasn't.*

'Come on,' Jeff urged them. 'We haven't got far to go.'

Soon a decent sized basketball court greeted them, both ends minus their baskets. On the white backboards (now grey with grime) more graffiti was evident, this species lighter in tone than the library's obscenities. *MR SHAMAN SUCKS BALLS!* read the left. And, no doubt penned by the same author, the right one proclaimed: *GOD ISN'T REAL. ABANDON ALL HOPE.*

'Thar she blows,' Jeff said, and pointed.

The cleaning closet sat to the right, its doorway almost completely camouflaged, having been painted the same bilious green as the wall. Of course, the same pattern repeated itself all over the school: students and faculty did not like to be reminded they procured mess, let alone required underlings to dispose of it. Although not full of yuppies per se, a subtle hint of snobbish mentality had always run through the school like an unspoken edict. Walking over, Jeff became acutely aware Dillion's camera was now focused entirely on him. This was, after all, his territory. His moment to shine.

'We always had a high turnover of cleaners,' he said, speaking loudly so the camera caught his words. 'We had immigrants, of course, every school has them. And even though some of them could hardly speak a word of English, I always found they were the hardest of workers, those that weren't proficient in the art of five-finger discounts, anyway. The university types were another story – every one of *them* had an aura of entitlement. Figured they didn't have to do the shitty jobs like the rest of us. Toilets were off limits, and if there was an unflushed crapper somewhere, then somebody with skin darker than theirs could take care of it.'

The cleaning closet had arrived. Anticipating it locked, Jeff was surprised to see its door handle missing. A half-inch gap gave evidence they would have unhindered access. 'Well, what do you know. It's open. Mr. Dillion, you won't be needing that crowbar after all.'

'I told you I was bringing one?'

'You did.' Jeff nodded. 'Told me the night you came up to my house.'

Alyssa said, 'So I guess we have a weapon after all.'

Jeff coughed, felt the small bulge of the pistol through the fabric of his trench coat.

No need to tell them yet. Not unless you need to pull it out, anyway.

With a quick glance at the others he raised his torch. Then, leaning in slowly, Jeff edged open the door of a cleaning room he had not entered since the event of Marcy Ribald over fifteen long years ago.

Though a decade of water damage had reduced the room to a washed-out husk, there was a moment (as the five of them crossed the threshold), where nothing had changed at all. Mounted along the walls, vacuum cleaners clung from steel pegs and water buckets were grouped on shelves. Heaped on the floor were dozens of cardboard boxes containing everything from fresh toilet paper to garbage bags, and a multitude of mops grouped in one corner with their respective heads missing. Still with lanyards attached, keys to different sections of the school lay heaped in a ceramic bowl by the entrance. Jeff blinked, and the illusion quickly evaporated. Taking its place, the secular rot infusing everything in the school outside.

'Christ, it stinks in here,' Alyssa said. 'This was your staff room, Jeff?'

Do I detect a subtle note of sarcasm, my dear?

'Kind of,' he replied. Straight ahead stood a buffing-machine encrusted with spider webs and, Jeff saw, many spiders. Fat daddy long-legs and one medium-sized black widow. 'It's where I kept the books; it's where we met at the beginning of each shift in the afternoon and where we signed off at night.'

Larger than an average cleaning closet, the space had

originally been designed to house a first-aid room. The principal, far too lazy to make the journey here, had then shifted the facility closer to the staff rooms. Cleared out and refurbished, two additional wash-sinks and an array of wooden shelves were then installed. After Jeff took over duties as site manager, the room became his home away from home; a small fortress for five days out of every week.

Dillion slapped his duffel bag on the concrete and began rummaging around.

'What are you doing?' Jeff asked him, pointing his beam directly on the man's scalp.

'There's no working light,' Dillion said. 'So I brought these. Here, each of you take one and place it on something in the corner.'

As if pulling an object from a hat, the director produced a wad of fat white candles, at least a half-a-dozen of them tied neatly together with twine.

'You're shitting me,' Alyssa said. 'You couldn't have told us about these earlier?'

'There was no need for them earlier.' Unwrapping the twine, Dillion proffered the sticks of wax. 'If you'd be so kind to light them up please, Alyssa?'

Alyssa accommodated, making sure one of her cigarettes were sparked up in the process.

Five stuttering candle flames floodlit the room.

Revealed was a smorgasbord of abandoned cleaning equipment and other objects (much like outside) that appeared to have had no rightful place in this room. On one shelf a mosaic of different-sized doll heads were arranged in neat compact lines, some of them still attached to vanilla torsos and sprouting filthy hair. Over toward the rear sat a decomposing black piano, its array of white keys like mottled human teeth.

Jason said, 'Do you think someone squats in here, too?'

Near the middle of the room a dilapidated trainset covered with an assortment of children's toys perched on a table. Stuffed teddy bears, Jeff noticed. And even what looked like a calliope jack-in-the-box with a grinning clown's face painted on the side. Underneath, a solitary Rubik's Cube sat atop a rubber tire the size and weight of a truck's spare.

Holding her candle out like a penitent, Carolina said, 'No. There's accumulated dust on everything here as well.' She giggled, an almost mad sound. 'It *does* look like some kid's nest, though. Look over there.'

Following her candle, Jeff spied a small squad of child-sized BMX bicycles; some fitted for girls, others for boys. More spider-webbing covered their rusted flanks. Dillion, no doubt sensing additional production value, walked over and began filming them.

The trainset had claimed Jeff's attention.

With an almost languid gait, he sauntered over toward it. Of course, it wasn't the trainset itself that fascinated him, more its position in the room. For it was the center or thereabouts where Marcy Ribald's body had finally been discovered. Splayed out on the dirty floor within a chalk pentagram she'd drawn herself, her interest in the occult augmented and increased exponentially by the unseen world.

Dillion had noticed his almost glazed look. 'Are you

ready, Jeff?' he asked.

Jeff looked at each of his companions in turn, the candlelight making serpentine shadows across their cheeks and foreheads. They stared back, expectantly, a willingness to listen but wholly unreconciled to the consequences of further reveals.

Sliding over a nearby cardboard box, Jeff sat down on it.

Then he began to tell his story.

'She was just like any of the other youngsters when first joining our team – nervous, new to the working environment and a little shy. I don't think I'm being politically incorrect by calling her a Goth, or an outcast, or a dye-your-hair-purple-and-black emo who was no stranger to ink on her ankles and listened to Marilyn Manson through her ear buds. Some of the older cleaners ribbed her a little during that first week – older men like Trevor Dinklage who always did a bit of hazing to see how far they could push a newbie. But that didn't last long once they discovered how kind she was. One of the great things about cleaning, about the *job*, is a person can be left to their own devices for the duration of a shift. If you're a loner by nature, it's a great gig. It was only during the holiday cleans we came together as a team, so the chance of getting on each other's nerves or prolonged harassment was a rare thing. We'd had one suicide, Matthew Thrane, but that boy already had a history of depression. At first I didn't foresee I'd have any problems with Marcy.'

'What year was this?' Dillion asked.

This was not the real Dillion asking, Jeff mused. *This was the documentary maker, kicking ass and taking down names.*

Jeff looked directly into the camera. 'In the fall of 2000. One way for me to gauge time was never things happening at the school, believe it or not. It was the music the kids were listening to. Rock bands were out, and boy bands were back in. That I remember.'

'And you said she was … initially kind?'

Nodding, Jeff said, 'Kind as a sister's kiss, despite her outward appearance. Quiet, too. Took her a few days to settle into the routine and make sure the sinks in the science building were done properly, but after that she was fine. Never took a sick day, either. Unlike how some of the others did on payday so they could go somewhere and drink it up.'

'I remember the papers,' Jason said. He stood by the door, as if ready to make a sudden exit if the situation demanded it. 'They said she started … grooming some of the adolescents during her shift?'

'Even now it's hard for me to believe it – to believe it was the same girl. Tuesdays and Thursdays she did the music room, the toilets downstairs, and emptied the trashcans on the second floor a bit later. She took a lot of time to do it, too. Forty-five minutes to be exact. *Too* much time in her four-hour shift. And just like in the gym, there's still a lot of students hanging around in that building after the final bell rings – students finishing up on their piano lessons, prepping the theater room, or just hanging around bored for their parents to pick them up.'

Dillion said, 'So she just … started making

conversation with the students?'

'We didn't encourage it. Talking to the faculty and students is somewhat forbidden, outlined as a no-no in the initial employment contract we sign, but everyone did it. You have to keep the lines of communication open so you knew when to clean the desks and when not to – when to stay out of the way if the teachers were conducting interviews with the parents and so forth. Marcy, I guess, liked to play the guitar at home, and during her clean she would pick up an instrument and get talking to the young ones. After all, it was only a short time ago she'd been one of them.'

Carolina looked confused. 'She was a student here, too?'

'No, I didn't say that.' Though he tried, it was difficult to keep the impatience out of his voice. 'I just meant she was fresh out of high school, herself. Had all the same concerns they did. During those nights she struck up a friendship with a girl, one Regina White. Regina's parents worked late in the city and didn't come to pick her up until well after 6 o'clock. Marcy, she … she would invite her down into this room while they waited.'

Jeff stopped. He could see the others weighing the import of his words, reconciling what they had seen on their TV screens with what he was divulging now. And it had all happened right here, of course, in this room. Young Marcy had seduced a female student – cajoled her into doing deeds among the dirty rags and bottles of bleach. Deeds deemed not only unethical in the school's eyes, but against the law as well. Because Regina had been a minor, only fifteen years old. And there had been others as well …

Now Dillion moved closer, edging toward Jeff in a way that was almost creepy. And though Jeff knew what was coming, had agreed to omit no details, it still made him feel as if he were disclosing something he shouldn't. 'Tell us what you know,' Dillion said.

'I caught them here, that first time. Came down to get a can of the bubble-gum remover – my trolley had run out – and I almost walked in on them. They were … going at it, I guess you could say. And Regina seemed entirely reciprocal from where I was standing. They didn't notice me watching, didn't hear my key slide through the lock. Marcy had cleared away what was in the middle and laid down some kind of a sheet for them. She'd also drawn something like a pentagram around it. Had her little stereo playing, too. The most horrible sounds you ever heard. Not like her death metal, either, but something even worse, something like chanting. Anyway, I quickly closed the door and slipped out. It was hard finishing up my part of the building, but I did it. Later, I came down and confronted Marcy.'

If there was even the slightest titillation amongst his audience, they chose not to reveal it. Jason appeared sick. Alyssa and Carolina the same. Dillion had not shifted from his rigor-mortis director's stance.

'She appeared shamed, of course. Utterly beside herself with it. Seemed perplexed, too, as if she had no recollection of having sex in this cleaning closet while she was supposed to be working. And do you know what? I don't believe she *did* remember. Not properly, anyway. You see, I'd been working here long enough to know how the unseen world could work on a person, and if it wanted to it could drive you a little crazy … or make you have strange desires you would *never* contemplate on an ordinary day.'

Dillion asked, 'The unseen world?'

Jason said, 'Strange desires?'

For this part Jeff suddenly found it difficult to look directly at his spectators. Instead, he stared down at the concrete. 'It's hard to explain. Like I told you before, there are a lot of nights a cleaner is completely alone. And it's at those times when you can feel the place working on you, *burrowing* into you. Myself, I thought I had developed a knack for tuning it out. But sometimes I let my guard slip. One night I almost went postal, wanted to trash the seventh grade science rooms and let out some of the nocturnal animals they kept bundled up in cages. And I almost did it, too –'

'The unseen world,' Dillion pressed.

'I haven't really mentioned that before now, have I? No, I guess not. Was kind of a personal nickname I gave to the *other* place overlapping this one. A place far-removed from the world of playing children and teachers but so close on some days you could almost smell it.'

'You didn't fire her then and there?' Alyssa asked.

'No, I didn't,' Jeff replied simply. 'Because I knew it wasn't really her. I did give her a warning, though. We had the same rules here as anywhere else. Three strikes and you're out. I told her romantic shenanigans were fine and good and none of my business … but that she needed to keep that stuff private and keep it at home.'

Jason's look of pale sickness had gravitated to outright revolt. 'But surely you knew it was more than just two girls

... *exploring* each other. What about the pentagram? The weird music you said she was playing?'

'We all carry guilt, Mr. Wedle. Some more than others. Why didn't you alert the school principal when Father Parrington began showing his illness physically? Weren't weeping sores enough for you to run to your mother and confess?'

For a moment Jason appeared dumbstruck, kneading his purple tie with one sweaty hand and staring at Jeff reproachfully. Then his shoulders slumped in resignation, and he nodded.

'I can't tell you why I didn't take more forceful action. I wanted the girl to keep her job, but it was probably more than that. Maybe I just wanted to see something like that again, or maybe, just *maybe*, Providence Place made me believe there would somehow be consequences if I breathed a word of it to anyone.'

Alyssa, using the trainset for an ashtray, butted out her smoke on the tracks and ignited another from her seemingly endless stash. 'But she kept doing it, didn't she?' she said. 'Kept bringing girls down here?'

'From what I later found out, yes. And boys, too. When students were interviewed in the ... shall we say aftermath, some of them confessed to a threesome taking place. Truth be told, I don't know absolutely everything that Marcy did.' Pausing, he added: 'Only what she did at the very end.'

At this, Dillion *did* move, scooting forward toward Jeff with the eerie agility of a stalker. Though Jeff recoiled, slightly taken aback, he took a deep breath and gathered the rest of his courage. This was, after all, what Dillion had paid him for.

'I got a call from one of my other cleaners, Robb, who'd finished his three-hour shift at 7:00 PM. He couldn't get into this room to return his key and sign out. Someone had jammed the door from the inside. Coming down the steps, I think I instinctively knew that whatever was happening to Marcy had reached a whole new level. A Matthew Thrane kind of level. Thankfully almost every child had disappeared by then, the only ones left were a few stragglers playing basketball in the northern quadrangle. I told Robb that when I opened the door, he wasn't to scream or make a scene. And he didn't, either – full credit to the man. Though he *did* quit the following day. No surprises there.'

'How did you get the door open?' Dillion asked.

'With a crowbar. Just like the one you've got in your bag. Took a while – Marcy had propped up one of the classroom chairs in need of fixing under the door handle. But we got it open ... eventually.

'There were three of them – four including Marcy. Although that was something else I didn't know until later. Because there were so many jostling limbs within the circle she'd drawn. Nylon clad legs and arms, some of them with their shoes still attached. Two girls and a boy. I couldn't see their heads at first, since they were underneath you see. But I could see their torsos, their intestines, and even shiny bone fragments like something you'd see in a butcher's window.'

'Jesus,' Carolina remarked, and Jeff noted the wince from Jason. A grown man whose cassock-wearing days were a thing of the past, he still carried the ability to recognize sin and disprove of it.

'I didn't notice Marcy for some time, because I was too numb with shock. That, and trying to figure out how she'd done it. I mean, there was a saw off to one side on my desk, still dripping blood, and various other cutting tools. But how had she managed to kill so quickly and efficiently? This was ... not just dismemberment; it was evisceration. The kind of skilled workmanship you'd expect a meat-packer or a fucking serial killer to perform.'

Jeff was out of breath, and he hated himself for it. Not all that long ago, (when Dillion had first made his offer), he had proclaimed to their director Providence Place didn't scare him like it did others. But what a cuntish joke that was turning out to be. Because here he sat on the cusp of hyperventilating. Those bodies had been *children* for Christ's sake; intact pieces of upright humanity with both personality and soul. And one of *his* cleaners had reduced them to something one might glimpse strolling through an abattoir: off-cuts of offal dumped unceremoniously into a boiling vat.

On the verge of hyperventilating or not, he certainly had their attention now. All that was really left to divulge was the state of Marcy herself.

Pointing a finger into the corner, he said, 'She jumped from over there.'

The others followed the path of his finger, eyebrows arched.

'I'd set up a small pyramid of crates – we used them sometimes to dust higher ground, places the adjustable mops couldn't reach. For most of the school year they just sat there, doing nothing. But Marcy put them to use.'

'She jumped?' Jason asked. 'You mean she hung herself?'

'Not precisely, no. She just jumped. But first, she placed a broom in her center, inside of her, so that when she came down, she landed on it. When I found her, she was sort of lying in a fetal position on her side. The broom had gone all the way through her body and come out her throat.'

Silence greeted the revelation. A silence, Jeff mused, that had substance. They were eyeing the crates, trying to imagine this grisly scenario playing out – trying to envisage the pain and *end result* of such a scenario. There were many ways a person could choose to end their life, countless means depicted on the news and shown in movies, but Marcy Ribald's selected method had a taboo, almost urban-legend mystique. Something you might have heard or read about but never dared to believe had actually played out.

'Most of it was covered up, of course. We did a lot of that here. Not the murders – you all know Marcy went crazy and killed herself and others. But let's just say there were no open casket memorials for the victims. And let us also say the school board paid out handsomely to their families in return for discretion.'

Again, there was more silence. But it didn't last long.

Outside, somewhere very close, another scream tore through the night.

SIX

It wasn't a woman screaming, Carolina thought. Not this time. This was vaguely feline ... or perhaps even the blaring of an infant.

Sometimes it was hard to differentiate between the two.

She recalled, sometimes with brutal clarity, the sound little Maddox had made in the often traumatizing days following his birth: a yowl like a Siamese cat in the initial stages of battle; a needy caterwaul signifying another feeding was imminent.

After Jeff's tale the group had reconvened back to the basketball court, Carolina more than happy with the unexpected interruption and a chance to vacate the suddenly oppressive cleaners' room. She was aware people had died in there, of course – had died *brutally*. But somehow Jeff's closing epilogue had given the past a new dimension. Where there was a trainset, Carolina could now see bodies. Where there were boxes, blood.

'It's moving away from us,' Dillion said, sounding mildly relieved despite his obvious intention to capture something else on film. 'Heading toward the art buildings.'

'Then that's the way we go,' Carolina said.

She could feel their collective gazes, probing.

'What? It's where we were heading anyway. After that, we press onto the gym and then the swimming pool.'

Was that so hard to believe? That she wanted to get to the pool swiftly, and have her part in all of this done? She supposed it was. Jeff and Jason had borne witness to both murder and suicide at Providence Place – had, in effect, gotten up close and personal with it. But her own story was a little more convoluted in the particulars, a tale comprising both bullying and rape. Rape at the hands of an otherworldly predator, no less. Of course, the official story had only scratched the surface of things – and there could be little doubt the group suspected this.

Only Alyssa looked on the verge of speaking up. She opened her mouth, closed it … then averted her eyes away from Carolina's.

The skinny mole has no idea what to say to me, whether she should be sad or sorry. How often in life do bullies get to meet their victims again as grown adults? Not many, I'll wager. Alyssa Asterious is still a stubborn bitch, and I'll also wager a thing like remorse probably doesn't fit into her vocabulary at all.

Carolina pushed the thought away. There would be time for recriminations later, if they surfaced at all.

By an unspoken command they started walking again. Underneath the sound of shoes slapping pavement, Dillion's audible commentary was a barely discernible monotone. Words of phantom screams had turned into annotations about the weather and legible graffiti. For the first time this night, Carolina found herself wondering just what kind of film would bear fruit for Dillion's obscure project. Was this pilgrimage a documentary to be sold to the highest bidding distributor? Or was it a series of weblogs for a ghost hunting website? From the outset, Dillion Cook had provided scarce details of his plight, his offer of payment in advance was more than enough incentive to convince Carolina to sign on the dotted line. Only months after she'd given up Maddox for adoption, her mother had forsaken Cranston altogether, essentially abandoning her. Shortly thereafter, both her father and brother had followed suit. Though the desertion had begun well before Maddox's arrival; had begun, in fact, the night of her attack. Although Sarah Gates had attempted enrolling her daughter in other places of learning, no local institute wanted to touch the pudgy swimmer whose listless countenance had graced a slew of *National Enquirer*-type publications. At first, Carolina had been grateful for the money and attention, could envision an end to a lifetime of bullying and harassment at the hands of students and teachers alike. But she should have known better, of course; should have known that once her perfectly normal baby entered the world, all offers to tell her story would dry up along with the promised money doing so procured. Soon enough Carolina's tale of a poltergeist became yesterday's headline, and the local media found some fresh horror at Providence Place to latch on to.

The basketball court ended, and another playground took its place. Happily entitled *Kurrajong* (taken after an

Australian tree which grew on the periphery), the space was an open education center where some of the younger children had amassed each day. Here, outdoor playing equipment in the form of swing-sets and mountable forts had shared space with sandpits and slides, a swath of land that had to be crossed by the older students to reach the arts center. Though some of the rides remained intact, others had succumbed to defacement, a miniature pyre erected and burned like a macabre offering. On the rear wall flanking the yard, a weathered sign proclaimed:

Childhood Should be a Journey, Not a Race.

Alyssa snorted. 'Well isn't that rich? *Now* they tell me. If only this had been erected when I was here, perhaps my life would have turned out differently.'

Carolina eyed her curiously. 'Do you still do any acting, Alyssa?'

In lieu of a reply, another cigarette was kindled. Then Alyssa caught wind of the others also watching her. 'Sometimes,' she answered, her tone almost defensive. 'Commercials, mostly. Last year I did a film-clip for a local band.'

'I remember it,' Jason said. 'For Lucid Dream, right?'

Alyssa blew out smoke, arched her eyebrows.

'Oh, I know what you're thinking,' Jason said. 'Not my kind of thing, right? You're forgetting I grew up singing in a choir. Lots of boys who grow up singing in a choir end up in the music scene.'

'Really? That a fact?'

'From my experience, yes.'

'You played in a band?'

'Not exactly. But some of my friends did. I went to a few shows during my university days. Lucid Dream was great. Still is.'

Carolina tried to imagine Jason sidled up to a bar and found she couldn't quite do it.

With flashlight beams straddling the murk, Jason's face had turned pink yet again. In an embarrassed tone, he asked, 'Say, can I pinch one of those?'

Alyssa appeared bewildered until she saw him staring at the bulge in her jeans. 'You want a cigarette?'

'If that's okay. My girlfriend wouldn't approve, but she's not here, is she? Also, my nerves are beyond frayed.'

The young altar boy hooked up with a girlfriend. Another one hard to envisage.

'What's her name?' Alyssa asked, grinning. Proffering her pack toward Jason, she thumbed out a smoke.

'My girlfriend?' Uncertainly, Jason stepped forward and plucked the offering. 'Kristen. Kristin Cantrell. She lives in East Greenwich, with her parents. When we get married, I'm going to move in with her there. She … doesn't like it here. She doesn't approve.'

Alyssa held out a wick of flame. 'You're going to live with her parents?'

'Yes. Well, sort of. They would live in a secondary unit out back.'

And just what does Kristen think of your adventure here tonight? Carolina thought but did not ask. Instead she said, 'Why doesn't she approve of Cranston?'

Jason inhaled his smoke, then coughed it out and grimaced. After a protracted silence staring at the thin cylinder distastefully, he said, 'This school, mainly. She says I should have moved away from Cranston as soon as I graduated. She says living so close to where so many people have died is morbid. I guess I would have to agree with her.'

Like a bullhorn's song, Jeff's voice cut through the chat. He had not uttered a word since the cleaners' closet. 'And why is that, do you think? Why have we all chosen to stay? From what Dillion here has told me, none of us live further than a twenty-minute drive. This, despite everything we've been through. This, despite everything we know.'

Always skulking, Dillion had crept up on them yet again. 'I think ...' he began, clearing his throat for the camera alone. 'I think I have another theory there. Is it that the place still has a hold on all of you, all these years later? Is it that you're afraid the ghosts will follow you, wherever you go? Is it that you've been waiting around for some kind of closure –'

'Oh, please,' Carolina said. 'Spare me. I stayed in Cranston because I don't have a goddamn choice. I stayed because I'm living in a public housing estate and can't afford to move. I came on a *bus*, remember? There's nothing mystical about all four of us still living here.'

'Careful,' Alyssa said, and tipped Carolina a sly wink. 'You'll spoil his fun.'

'No, he has a point,' Jason said, still hypnotized by the glowing ember perched between his joints. 'I don't know about you guys, but there's a part of me – a part that never switches off or seems to sleep – that's still getting up every morning and going to school here. The smell of the church, the sound of car doors slamming as parents drop off their kids – all those things are still so fresh it's like drying paint. When Mr. Cook – when Dillion came to me with his offer, part of me jumped at the chance. I *wanted* to come back. My pastor says you can't move on from a relationship until you confront and experience all of the ugly emotions that go with it, not hide from them. And I've had a relationship with Providence Place for as long as I can remember. Dillion calls it a returning … I prefer to think of it as *confronting*.'

Engrossed in the spiel, Carolina remained unaware of the newcomer in their midst. Not until it was too late. If she'd been on her usual guard, listening intently, she may have heard the dog's furtive movements or sensed its presence before it reached them.

Instead the mongrel waltzed into their circle almost lazily … a Doberman patterned with filth and dripping saliva from its maw, a feral thing that called Providence Place its home.

'Don't run,' Carolina whispered. 'For Christ's sake, don't anybody run.'

Although the bodiless creature in the locker had remained unknown, its anatomy debatable, there could be little doubt what confronted them now.

A dog.

Emaciated by considerable malnutrition, it padded toward them with stealth. Deep in its throat, barely audible, Carolina detected a growl.

From her left came a clicking sound, something sliding into place.

Alyssa said, 'Jesus Christ, Jeff – you brought a fucking *gun?*'

Jeff didn't reply, merely kept his eyes and pistol trained on the animal.

Dillion said, 'No, Jeff. Don't shoot the poor thing. It's probably scared as hell.'

'Does it *look* scared?' Jeff asked.

The dog let out a shrill bark, shifting its gaze from one individual to the next.

'Everyone lower your lights,' Alyssa said.

They did so, unconsciously taking small steps back as the animal came closer. Only ten feet away now, give or take. From this distance, Carolina could discern one eye completely covered in milky cataract. The other, black as oil, had now focused on Jeff, its ability to perceive a threat intact.

If all of us decide to bolt, it will zero in on one of us and succeed in the take down. If Jeff shoots it, we run the risk of somebody nearby calling the cops ...

Would that be the outcome here? Thus far, their journey stepping into Providence Place had the distinct feeling of being removed from the outside world. As far as Carolina knew, the real estate bordering the school was made up of featureless parklands with only a meager smattering of houses surrounding them. At least, that was how she remembered it ... and all she had seen on her walk from the bus stop earlier. If nearby residents *did* exist, they were more than likely to ignore anything coming from the direction of the school – especially anything reeking of violence. This was something pertinent that occurred during the place's heyday, teachers and students turning a blind-eye or even deigning to cover up anything they couldn't rationally explain.

'Here, boy,' Dillion said. Though still backtracking, he had somehow managed to liberate some snacks from inside his backpack. Fumbling with different packets, he struggled to remove their contents.

And the dog moved in.

Turning around, Carolina broke into a sprint, but her effort was cut short as Jeff's pistol uttered two short, round barks eclipsing the dog's own. Loathe to witness the carnage, Carolina could only stare at the cement, cradling her torch within a fold of tummy fat and breathing in long, heaving gulps. To her right, Dillion's bag slapped the concrete, its innards ejected. Also spilling out: a fusillade of harsh words aimed at the shooter, assurances Dillion would have soon won the moment.

'I'm sorry,' Jeff muttered. Finally finding the impetus to turn around, Carolina saw him standing limply by the creature's side. Being so close, the bullet had found its prize easily, tearing a sizeable chunk of matter from one side of its throat. Blood spouted from the ragged wound. Scooting closer, Carolina saw the ebbing wave of its stomach, its lungs still clinging to a fragile life.

'You killed it,' she muttered, as if giving authorship to the narrative would somehow make it more substantive, more real. 'You just … popped it. Didn't think to shout at it? Didn't even try to scare it off?'

'No, I didn't,' he said, and covered the remaining distance until he was kneeling beside one jittering paw. 'And I'll tell you why. Someone, please give me some light here.'

Too tired to object, Carolina watched in addled fascination as Jeff reached down and began to reposition the thing's head. By now, its midsection had ceased its undulations, while its legs no longer attempted the mimicry of a gallop. Even the blood flow seemed to have abated. As Jason's torch found Jeff's hands, Carolina recoiled. While the eyes had been mostly unobservable from a distance, Carolina saw they had now sunk deep within their sockets, yielding inward with a cadaverous drooping only a corpse in the latter stages of rigor mortis could produce.

Alyssa said, 'That can't be possible. Can it?'

Things only became more puzzling when Jeff pulled back one drool-adorned tarp of its muzzle; a snout that even now continued to degenerate. Gums, black and glistening, were host to two rows of gangrenous teeth unlike any Carolina had ever seen. *Like stumps of grey licorice* she thought morbidly. Seeing them, Jeff quickly dropped the head, wiping his hands on the pockets of his coat.

'What the fuck is it?' Dillion asked. At some stage he'd produced his crowbar, and delicately pushed back what Jeff had closed. All of them jumped when a hot bubble of blood and air escaped.

'I think it was a Doberman, once,' said Jeff.

They stared at him, a wise old sage suddenly proficient in the mysteries of Providence Place.

'Let me guess,' Alyssa ventured. 'The unseen world?'

He shook his head, bloodshot eyes within his dark sockets downcast. In the halogen wake of their torches, his countenance appeared spectral, as erudite as any old prophet. 'Like Mr. Dillion here, I can only postulate. When it came at us, it's like I saw something lurking underneath, a rippling along the side of its coat. For a split-second I thought it may be infected with something … then I noticed some of its ribs sticking out, though they weren't sticking out from starvation. I could see them whole.'

As if in mock benediction to Jeff's statement, the dog's stomach made a series of digestion sounds, then its lower portion collapsed under a weight of pressure. More gas belched out.

'So what are you saying?' Jason asked incredulously. 'That it's some kind of a … ghost dog?'

Another shake of the head. Jeff was like a teacher at the scene of an autopsy. 'Not that … not precisely, anyway. We all saw that thing in the locker.'

'Go on,' Dillion said. 'Spill it. Tell us what you're thinking.'

'First, let's all take a step back.'

No one asked why. The dog – what was left of it – had begun its last transcendent stages, liquefying under the duress of a process that would be deemed unnatural under any microscope. When it was done, the only evidence of its existence were voluminous teeth arrayed around a grey brooding sac of flesh.

Jeff said, 'There were similar things years ago, I'm sure of it now. Stray cats and dogs who wandered in at night and never wandered back out, mostly during the holidays when it was vacant. I noticed them scampering around and trailing their strange second-selves. I remember ringing pest control a few times … now I wonder what the final result was when they piled them into the truck. Did those vets see the same thing I did? Like they were walking skeletons but not quite? I can't say. Alyssa, you asked me

before if this is a manifestation of the unseen world.
Perhaps, in a certain way it is. Perhaps that's *exactly* what it
is.'

'Great, so there's probably more of them out here?'
said Alyssa. 'Dillion, I'm starting to think this might be
beyond my pay grade. If you want us all to hang around,
that is.'

Absorbed in the task of filming the steaming carcass,
Dillion ignored her, making more observations as he did so.
At last, content with whatever he had, he turned around to
face them. 'We're off schedule –'

'We have a schedule?' Carolina asked.

'Not precisely, no, but we're running late if we want to
get to your story by midnight. Whatever's out there, you all
signed a legal document. No one leaves until filming is
complete. That's if you want to get the second lump
payment, of course.' He looked back at the carcass, licked
his upper lip once. 'Cheer up, people. This is hard stuff I
have on film. The kind of thing that will put us all on the
map.'

The art center was exactly as Carolina had anticipated:
the kind of chaos reserved for a future dystopia. While the
crux of the walls remained intact, the interior itself was a
hodgepodge of deteriorating trash. Here all the contents of
an art studio (easels, paints, and pottery) had been given a
hellish afterlife as a ruined photographer's dream. While
the journey over and inspection of the bottom floors had
been for the most part uneventful, scaling the stairs to the
second story was proving a calamitous obstacle course of

rotting machinery and shattered glass.

Carolina, her insides already famished, could feel her hunger reaching a boiling point. It didn't help that she knew what Dillion carried inside his backpack besides a crowbar and other cameras. There were snacks like Pringles. And chocolate. She'd seen them topple out immediately after the dog had launched itself.

But I won't give into asking for them, she thought.

I can't. Not with Alyssa here.

Why the hell not? the voice of hunger spoke up. *He brought them for that very reason. Also, why do you give a shit what that bitch thinks of you now?*

About to plunge into further debate, her thoughts were put on hold as the group, now walking in single file up the stairs with Carolina taking up the rear, came to a stop. They'd done this a few times already, Dillion pausing as some kind of hurdle presented itself on the steps. Ahead, the glow of Jason's flashlight bobbed like a singular eye.

Minutes passed with no instruction.

'What is it?' Alyssa called from somewhere in the middle.

'We have to turn around,' Dillion called back.

'What? Why now? We're almost to the top.'

No reply. For a while the only sound was their collective, exhausted breathing. Not answering was one thing, but for Dillion to propose turning around when their quarry was near meant that whatever was blocking their passage was shitty in the extreme.

'Just … I think we have to turn around.'

Being fearful notwithstanding, that comment was enough to pique Carolina's interest. Bad enough to just hightail it back? Her mind wondered what kind of horror lurked on the stairs.

'Let me see,' Alyssa said, obviously having the same thought.

Though Dillion tried to warn her away the closer she came, Alyssa wasn't going to be denied. A small melee of arguing broke out, but it was quickly stifled. Carolina waited, poised. After a while Jason began moving to join them, and Carolina, despite her trepidation, quickly followed.

Can't be any worse than a mannequin full of rats, she thought, and felt a shiver course through her back. *And whatever you do, don't freak out this time – don't jump up out of harm's way like someone in a Bugs Bunny cartoon ...*

Three steps later and the dead girl hove into view. Though far from a skeleton, decomposition had set in long ago, transforming her overall visage into that of a mummified Egyptian. Skin – stretched like pelt – still clung to her face, a brown leather mask. Her fingernails were long, as was her hair, the most obvious sign of her sex. Her arms were splayed out, twin palms stretched toward the newcomers as though seeking their aid.

'Oh, my God,' Jason whispered. 'She died trying to get through.'

This appeared to be correct. Wedged between a bulky table and some kind of printing press, the girl had been in the process of moving herself through a thin crevasse where the two monstrous items came together. Her midsection (sporting a still-intact fawn woolen jumper) was a mishmash of skin and fabric, scrapes and welts; the ideographic scars etched by the objects trapping her. The others, having parted to the side like a proverbial sea to accommodate Carolina, simply stared on in awestruck shock. Then Jason pulled out a cell phone from one of his pockets.

'What are you doing?' Dillion asked.

'What do you think I'm doing? Calling the police.'

'No, not yet. We have to think about this.'

'What's to think about? There's a dead girl in front of us.'

Reaching out his hand, Dillion placed it on Jason's wrist, effectively blocking his ability to dial. 'And in all likelihood that was a crime scene back in the library. But we didn't call the police then, and we aren't going to now.'

Though their faces were dark silhouettes, Carolina had no trouble making out Jason's horrified expression. 'But she's *dead*. That's a dead body. She got trapped on the top floor and tried to get out … oh boy, she most likely died of starvation. That's somebody's *daughter*. We have to call the police.'

'And we will,' Dillion said. 'I promise you, we will. Once filming is completed. She's been here for years, Jason. She isn't going anywhere now.'

Bringing her flashlight back up, Carolina shone it directly into the cadaver's mouth – a dark hollow filled with stalactite teeth. *Tooth bacteria causing dental decay doesn't survive in a dead body*, she thought crazily, a long dormant science lecture surfacing with brutal clarity. *After a person's death the teeth become one of the most durable parts of the body ...*

'She was screaming,' Alyssa said, her voice sounding

sick and resigned. 'She died screaming. That's why her mouth is opened so wide.'

As they watched, Dillion began filming her – first slowly, then zeroing in on her face … then finally gliding over her body with the same dexterity he'd shown shooting everything else. Despite Carolina's revulsion in the act, there was an undeniable fascination watching him at work.

'No goddamn decency at all,' Jason muttered, and they all looked at him, including Dillion, who stopped his labor completely. Although Jason had appeared distraught many times – particularly during his tale – Carolina had assumed the man incapable of properly cursing. *There's one good thing about this*, she thought. *I've lost my fucking appetite.*

Dillion said, 'Perhaps if we move some of the debris, climb over her –'

'No freaking way, Dillion,' Alyssa said. 'You've had your fun. This is a dead end. Time we got moving again.'

By way of reply, Dillion gave a forlorn sigh. For a while he stood his ground, camera lowered, then nodded in acquiescence. This close, Carolina thought she caught her first whiff of the cadaver … an emission like moth-balls and rotting banana peels, of dead flowers and time.

It's my first dead body. That's why I can't look away.

And as Carolina made the first move to leave, turning her back and illuminating the staircase once more, some fundamental voice insisted it wouldn't be her last.

It was with a stoic kind of resolve the group mounted the steps to what had, during the reign of Carolina's years, been officially branded the Heartwood Swim Center. Eight lanes with a year-round temperature of 78 degrees Fahrenheit. Or so it had liked to boast. Occasionally opened to the general public on weekends, the center had claimed the crowning jewel of the school's annual budget. While the arts often suffered (as they did in most metropolitan schools), each successive principal only had to point out the level of achievement Providence Place had when it came to athletics.

Carolina Gates had, for a time, been one of them.

Taking to the water as a mere babe, her lack of social relationships and shortcomings in academia were enough to cement long hours immersed in water when others were about more collective pursuits. Though her initial attempts at competing were disparaged by her family, they slowly came around when blue ribbons and trophies, not time spent in a pool, soon became the order of the day. After participating in the World Junior Championships in Los Angeles in 1988, it wasn't long before her coaches looked toward entering in major meets once her high-schooling days were over. Looking at the front façade now, it was hard to imagine those giant glass doors were the same ones that had ushered her through mornings and nights into a place smelling of chloramines, perspiration, and discipline. On top of the doors, only a few letters remained of the original Heartwood sign with *Heart* erased completely. In its place somebody – perhaps the same individual who'd defaced the basketball boards – had scribbled the word: *Worm*.

'Wormwood Swim Center,' said Alyssa. 'Has a nice ring to it.'

Carolina's heart ached at the sight. Though she'd

wholly expected this, seeing it was another thing … akin to witnessing a childhood home razed to the ground. Despite her story ending in a kind of tragedy, her fondest memories would always be synonymous with the swim center. The type where she had left all her insecurities behind and taken flight in a vacuum of water.

'Stay close to each other,' Dillion told them. 'Join our beams together to make a single path. There's liable to be a shitload of broken glass everywhere.'

They did so, Alyssa making an idle quip about crossing the streams in reference to the movie *Ghostbusters*. 'We even have a token black dude,' she said as they walked, and laughed uproariously.

Jeff did not laugh in turn.

While the top portion of the building was shaped somewhat like a dome (hundreds of glass skylights permitting the sun to blaze through during the day), the lower region was a small warren of metal blockades to herd a considerable crowd when championship meets took place at the school. Navigating them, Carolina had the distinct impression of an iron labyrinth gone to rust and abandoned by its architects. Briefly, the image of the dead teenager trapped in her own maze tried to resurface … and she quashed it before it could mature.

Once in the building the pool made itself known, a black void the size and width of a small airplane hangar. On their right, a dust-mote laden passageway petered off into a myriad row of shower stalls and change rooms. To the left, stadium seating shared space with conference rooms walled off by see-through glass partitions. With the conjoined might of their flashlights, only brief patches of the interior were revealed in stark detail.

Ambling toward the pool, Jeff said, 'Do you hear that?'

Silence as they listened. From up high, Carolina detected a soughing of wind through obvious holes in the glass roof. Then she heard it: a gurgle of water like the rush of a stream.

'The pool?' Jason inquired. 'Surely there's no water left in it?'

Treading lightly they made their way toward the edge. Almost tip-toeing, Carolina mused. Just before the raised piece of concrete slab heralding the brink, Dillion held out an arm, keeping them from taking another step further. Lowering her light, Carolina peered into the inky well.

At first there was nothing: pale, insubstantial shapes of debris. *Floating* debris. The water, though filling only a portion of the pool, was a grey morass of churning sludge. Following Dillion's light, Carolina spied a fountain of water spurting from plumbing about halfway down the bottom.

In a low-pitched lilt, Alyssa sang, 'You left the *water* running ...'

Bristling, Carolina swung her light into Alyssa's face.

'What, not an Otis Reading fan?'

'I can't make out any of this stuff,' Jason said. 'What *is* it?'

Pushing past Dillion's arm, Jeff said, 'There's something huge in the deeper end.'

'There's a deeper end?' Jason asked.

'Depth for the diving boards,' Carolina replied automatically. A question she'd fielded numerous times over the years, she could feel Jason nodding in comprehension.

Excited, Jeff had moved off into the darkness ahead. Soon the point of his light came to rest about fifty feet away, more or less in line with the ladders broaching the diving dais. Then it descended as Jeff took to his hands and knees, inspecting his find. Making her way over, Carolina could envision an entire pool full of corpses identical to the girl in the art center, bodies stacked atop each other like cordwood.

Or like something from a World War II era reel, her mind spoke morbidly. *A pit of arms, torsos, and malformed legs. Every head pulled back in a rictus smile of –*

'I don't believe it,' she heard Jeff say as they joined him. He was still on his haunches, looking almost ready to leapfrog off.

It took Carolina some courage to get closer to the edge, her own light making inroads into the detritus below. First there was a wedge of something yellow, then the jarring silver oblong of a machine-grill, and finally two headlights canted up on an angle but staring up at them. Before long Carolina ascertained she was staring at the derelict remains of a school bus.

One of the school's yellow buses sitting in the bottom of the hollow pool.

'I can believe it because I'm looking at it,' Alyssa said. 'But how did it *get down* there?'

'How did anything get where we've seen it? Jason replied. 'Like that church bell on the balcony? If somebody *drove* the bus into the pool, it would be totaled. Like, a Tonka toy smashed to pieces.'

Trailing her beam along the bus's roof, Carolina became aware of a hole in the middle, a perfectly spherical opening festooned with rust. *As if someone just poured a barrel of fucking acid on the spot.* For a moment the world swam, and she felt her frame sway sluggishly forward. Then she felt Jason's hand steel her back.

'Are you all right?' he asked. 'Somebody help me out here.'

'No, no. I'm fine,' she said. 'It's just ... my mind's trying to reconcile *this* place as the same one I swam in every day. And I can't do it. It's like they're two separate worlds.'

Dillion said, 'Hold that thought. Perhaps it's time for you to take a seat, Carolina.'

A second passed where Dillion's words may have been spoken in another language. Then it dawned on her: she had returned here for a very specific reason.

She had returned to tell a tale.

Though Carolina had protested, more candles were set up, and by their light the group sat in a rough circle on the stadium seating. Positioned about halfway up the tiers, the candlelight created a beige womb of warm light that felt like protection, even if it was of a meager sort. Everything outside the light – the unseen glass roof, the dark chasm of the pool itself – was like an overpowering miasma, one that could almost be perceived on an emotional level. And though Carolina had stated coming back was like returning to a different world, the past still felt ever present ... like the background static of radio tuned to a midnight frequency.

While Dillion prepared his camera, Jason passed around the chocolate bars and potato chips. Two-liter containers of Gatorade were also to be found in Dillion's bag.

'Why don't we just break out the booze?' Alyssa suggested.

Expecting a complaint from Dillion (their director would no doubt want his cast sober), Carolina was surprised to see the man consent when observing they all shared the same expectant look. After breaking the seal and taking a small swig to ascertain it was indeed as the label proclaimed, Jason handed the bottle to Carolina first, a wordless gesture she was perhaps deserving of its effects before anyone else.

'Tastes like a whole bunch of dead ants,' Jeff said after it was his turn to take a swig. 'Never had a taste for wine. Now beer – that's something I could happily bathe in.' Grimacing, he proffered the bottle to Dillion.

Already Carolina could feel the wine's trajectory through her stomach, a silken fire that clamored for more. The chocolate had felt wonderful, but this felt even better: a twin pillar of relaxant and confidence booster. She licked her lips, about to say something (though she didn't know what), when Dillion asked the question: 'Was it a ghost that attacked you that morning, Carolina?'

Put so bluntly, she could feel an unwelcome degree of self-consciousness returning. Again without saying anything, Jason had passed the bottle back into her hands. She drank.

'First, let's go back a bit,' she said. 'Before the day of

the so-called ghost.'

Four pairs of eyes watched her intently. No one interjected.

'Beginning in the winter of, this would be 1990, I began training in the mornings. I'm not sure if you remember Coach Mannering, or the rumors that had begun circulating about her –'

'That she was a rug-muncher?' Alyssa asked.

Carolina ignored her. 'But she resigned not long after. I trained five nights a week, but with no coach appointed as Mannering's replacement I could do what I liked.'

Dillion said, 'I tracked her down, believe it or not. She lives in Maine. Never went back to coaching, or teaching. Rumors like that can dog you for life, I suppose.'

Carolina wanted to say: *So does bullying, my dear.* Instead she simply nodded.

'It seems a bit of a cliché, for a swim teacher that is, but it happens all the time. And Coach Mannering looked the part. She had muscles, short blonde permed hair, and spent all of her time with younger female students. You're probably thinking, was she a lesbian? And the truth is I never really thought she *wasn't*. You could see it from space. But she never laid a finger on me or any other student.' Here she shot Alyssa a coarse look. 'The foul accusations usually begin with the most popular kids at school, and once they do, they spread like wildfire. Poor Coach Mannering never stood a chance.'

If Alyssa perceived an insult, her stoic face resolved not to show it.

'So you were in between coaches?' Dillion asked.

Carolina nodded. 'I liked getting to school early.

Hardly any students compared to those that stuck around at night. And the pool was all mine.'

'This school has always had a … questionable reputation,' said Jeff. 'Weren't you just a little bit scared being in here all by yourself?'

'Are you asking me whether I was ever aware of your unseen world, Jeff?' Transformed by the light of fluttering candle flame, Jeff's face resembled a hooded mask. 'I guess the answer to that would be yes. Nothing I ever saw with my own eyes, mind you. Just a feeling you would sometimes get coming up for air. Like someone was watching you. Every now and then it felt like something was *underneath* me, ready to drag me down underwater. I remember closing my eyes even though I wore those little goggles, just in case. But mostly I felt safe. I was free, you see. Free from the bullying names and Coach Mannering's drills.'

Almost without being aware of it, more wine had made it to her mouth. With each successive sip, her head began to sing in chorus with the warm feeling in her stomach. 'Until the morning of the 23rd of August, that was. When I was hard at it, one of the coach's techniques for freestyle involved imagining something behind us … something bad. Chasing us, if you will. Whether it be one of the teachers who were giving us grief, or whether you just wanted to imagine Godzilla himself swimming toward you to increase your speed, it was a method that worked for some and not for others. For me, not usually. But I remember using it on that particular morning. Stroking away, I tried to envision a great black blob of energy on my tail, slowly gaining. A thing that took up at least four lanes and had an appetite for young girls. And my imagination was up to the task, it seemed, because I could *see* it in my head, like a moving oil slick through the water. Soon afterward I could *feel* it. Feel its dark energy behind me. Enough so that I had to stop swimming and look around. Of course, when I *did* look around, treading water and panting, the thing was actually there, as real as all of you sitting before me.'

It was a narrative she'd dispensed many times, of course. In many different ways. But now lent gravitas by their proximity to the pool. Keeping his camera focused on her face, Dillion turned around and looked at it. So did the others. No one said anything, permission for Carolina to take up the reins of the past once more.

'At first I thought I was seeing things – you'd be surprised what physical exhaustion and chlorine can do to your brain when you're in the zone. But I could see it underwater, too. And I could *smell* it. Jeff, you would know the smell of the school well – it's like the smell of old bananas, teenagers' sweat, and bubble gum. It was all of those things but amplified beyond belief and getting stronger by the second.'

Alyssa, who up until now had been holding the captivated expression of somebody brainwashed, screwed up her nose in what was an obvious show of skepticism … perhaps outright disbelief. Jeff reached for the bottle clasped in her hands. Dillion eased his iPhone even closer.

'Though I wanted to turn around and keep swimming, I simply couldn't. It was paralyzing, seeing such a thing come at you. And make no mistake, it was *me* its sights were set upon. That feeling was almost as tangible as the sudden smell in the air. Like it had waited years for the opportunity, perhaps even generations. And now that I was close it wasn't going to be denied.'

'You keep saying *it*,' Dillion said. 'Do you mean this dark cloud or …?'

'The school? It was both. They were one and the same. The school was the cloud and the cloud was the school. Like I said, I was paralyzed, merely treading water on autopilot. Occasionally my head would dip under for just a moment, enough where I could open my eyes again, and the closer it came the more details I could make out.'

With a slight slur to her speech, Alyssa said, 'A merman?'

Though the core of his attention remained fixed on the tale-teller, Dillion deigned Alyssa a protracted glare. He said, 'You won't be having any more wine tonight.'

But Carolina wasn't about to be slowed now.

'I told the reporters back in the day it was like something from a movie … that sounds trite now, I know. Too convenient. But you have to understand this was before the era of computerized special effects. My imagination simply had no other reference point to catalogue it. It was everything you would expect to see in a horror film, yet at the same time infinitely worse. There were *things* inside that cloud. Hundreds of things. Like an entire ecosystem of them breaking through the surface layer of the cloud as it came through the water toward me. There were faces in that ecosystem, I think – but they were of such an alien magnitude it was like trying to understand bacteria if you were shrunk to its level and face-to-face with it. When it was close enough I only just managed to keep my eyes open. Then it entered me.'

Expecting guffaws from Alyssa, Carolina was surprised by the silence. For a while the only sound was the endless trickle of the spume in the pool.

'I'd like to say I blacked out here, or at least had some kind of amnesia concerning the next part, but that wouldn't be true at all. When offshoots of the cloud entered me, they entered where you would expect … in the same place where Marcy Ribald placed her broom. Up it went, through my system, filling every part, every cavity. At this stage my head was still above the surface, just, and I could see the bulk of the cloud had come to a complete stop. Part of my everyday brain was still conscious, and I remember thinking that whatever it was wasn't regulated to the water, because I could see those churning faces very clearly above the surface, breaking in waves of ecstasy or agony. And I'll tell you one other thing: I could *feel* them inside me, too. Feel them sniffing out my organs and riding the waves of my blood. Not human, I remember thinking. Whatever they were had *never* been human. But that's why they were here, you see, inside me; they wanted to understand what it was to *be* human.'

More quiet. This of the awed type. Whatever doubts any of them harbored were waylaid by a simple revelation: *Carolina* believed these things had happened to her. She was telling the truth as she understood it.

Dillion cleared his throat. 'If they weren't human … what do you think they were?'

Carolina shrugged. 'People always wanted the simple explanation – the dark cloud contained the ghosts of days gone by. Or whatever nonsense best suits the linear mind. I can only … Jeff, what word did you use before? I can only *postulate* what entered me that morning. Something cosmic; something different from things that live here. Something that was around long before the school was ever built. Don't you see? The school was built *around* this thing, or on it. In some ways we're the invaders encroaching on its turf. I felt that, too. Over a hundred years of studying us wasn't enough. So now, through me, it was going to do something completely different.'

Throat parched, Carolina lifted up the last dregs of wine from the bottle to her lips and swallowed. Licking them, she said, 'It was going to *use me* to see the world.'

Concerning that particular morning, there wasn't much else to tell. Not long after her encounter (a thing even worse with this telling), Carolina had succumbed to unconsciousness. Finally acceding to shock or being remedied into further paralysis by the entity she could not say. Only a short time later, a member of the teaching staff had found her floating on her back and drifting aimlessly. After diving in and retrieving her limp body, a greenhorn type of resuscitation had ensued. Though the act had been unnecessary, because Carolina had not ingested any water.

Only a monster.

Dillion asked, 'Do you remember anything at all during this period of unconsciousness?'

'Yes. And in some ways, what I saw during this period was even worse than being chased in the pool. It was like taking a small peek through the eyes of the faces in that cloud … how they saw the world at large. A kind of appetite, but not as we think of it. To them appetite is the most natural of things, an important base emotion. Devour everything and anything. If Providence Place was built around their home, a place where the walls are thin, then what they saw while the school was in full swing was a place where appetite could be indulged to the fullest. So much strange energy concentrated in one place, it was like a smorgasbord. Think about it – all the neuroses that come with puberty, all the creativity and insecurities of the very young. A concentrated cesspool for something that knows only appetite. Time moves at an entirely different level, too. No surprises there. No day or night in Jeff's unseen world, only an eternally dark moment where they can flit in and out of our lives like spectators.'

Dillion's camera now stood only inches from her face, and in the sudden torpor of the moment, Carolina felt no diffidence at its presence. *Let it hang there*, she decided.

'Appetite,' Dillion stated. 'Are you saying that they feed … fed on human beings?'

'Not on souls,' she said. 'Nothing so corny. More on our actions and emotions. The building itself is like something caught in a web. *Their* web. A web where strange creatures can be manipulated and even given a taste of their own burning appetite. They want us to suffer like they do.'

There was more, Carolina remembered. During that brief fugue state she had also glimpsed something like a city overlapping everything … a dark yet transparent metropolis infested with black clouds. But then she had woken, and most of it had sunk into the background like a half-remembered dream. It was only later – with Maddox coming to full term – that her full experience would come crawling back, every nuance to be relived over and over again. For now, she would glide over this small detail. However, one pertinent part of her story remained …

'As everybody knows, it was then I became pregnant. And yes, on that morning, I was a virgin. Nobody would date the walrus, let alone sleep with her. Even with my swimming accolades. Two weeks later, I missed my period; *three* weeks later, my breasts began to feel tender. I was sick as hell. About a month after that I got tested. Later, when I went to the hospital, a few local journalists followed me into the clinic. Can you believe that? The story had broken through no real fault of my own. When I was discovered floating and unconscious, I was understandably hysterical. I remember sitting in sick-bay with a towel wrapped around me, shivering, and I just spilled everything, all of it, hoping there would be some kind of rational explanation or somebody who could *help me.* What I didn't count on was the story reaching the ears of everyone on the playground during the first few days. If I was mocked before because of my appearance, I was *ridiculed* now.'

'I remember it,' said Jeff. He no longer stared at Carolina, preferring instead to study his hands. 'The two cleaners responsible for the gym and pool building asked to be transferred.'

'And that's what I found to be the most traumatic part of the experience in the aftermath. People made fun of me, but I knew, deep down, that most of the school *believed* me. Believed I saw something, anyway. Because everybody here – whether they admitted it to themselves or not – knew of this unseen world. Believe me, if you attended here every day, you just did. Most of the time it was like an annoying sound that hardly bothered you at all. But on some days it affected everyone, including those who harassed me afterward. I don't doubt for a second the place was working through them, too. Scaring the shit out of me and knocking me up wasn't enough. The school wanted to *brutalize* me.'

'And you really believe that now?' Dillion asked. Relieved, Carolina could tell this wasn't the man, but the commentator. 'That you were knocked up?'

She said, 'Eight months later little Maddox came into the world. Eight months during which I quit Providence Place altogether and decided to give interviews because I had nothing to lose. I was now a bona-fide high-school dropout. How the hell was I going to support the baby when it arrived? And sure, I hammed it up a bit for their cameras. It's what they asked for, after all.'

Eyes almost preternaturally accustomed to the dim light, Carolina could now see expressions far removed from those held when she'd first begun her tale. Whether it was because they had their own secrets to spill, or they were finally hearing it from the horse's

(walrus's)

mouth, the group now observed her guardedly. Even Alyssa's bravado seemed to have abated.

'Of course, the money only lasted so long. Appalled by my actions with the media, my mother disappeared. Then the rest of my family. I was all alone with a baby I never wanted.'

She had thought herself beyond tears; thought the last of them had dried up years ago. But here they were again. It was little Maddox, of course. Memories of spending time with him were still sharp. Candid up until now, Carolina realized she had just spoken her first lie. She *had* wanted to keep Maddox, for what it was worth.

She just couldn't give him the life he deserved.

Though she expected the next question to come from their director, Carolina was surprised when Jason finally gave it a voice.

'Did you have him tested when he was born?' he said to her. 'You know, a paternity test?' He paused, cleared his throat. 'What kind of ... behavior did the child exhibit?'

'You mean did he start puking green soup or talking in a demonic voice?' she asked. 'Did he look at the world around him as if he wanted to destroy it? Nothing so dramatic, I'm afraid. And no, I never had a paternity test. Maddox was named after my great-grandfather and showed all the signs of a normal, healthy, and functioning child. I wish I could give you something else here, some kind of proper closure. But there isn't much more to say. One-and-a-half years after he was born, I put little Maddox up for adoption and never saw him again. I have no idea who his parents are ... or even if he still lives in Rhode Island.'

'But how could you do that?' Alyssa asked. 'You thought the child was an offspring of the *school* and you just gave him up? How could you do that?'

'We're not here to judge, Allyssa,' Dillion said. Pocketing his phone, he picked up one of the stuttering candles. 'We're here to film a movie. Which, by the way, also includes an account of your own. We need to get moving again.'

Jason had picked up one of his own candles.

'Something is bugging me,' he said. 'This ... cosmic thing that Carolina mentioned. The things inside the cloud. If they fed on our actions and emotions, if they used *people* like puppets before the school closed, what are they feeding on now? Since arriving we've ascertained they're *still here*, aren't they? What have they been doing since the place turned into an urban wasteland?'

From the pool, a sound drifted over.

A mournful wail like the call of a loon.

'Oh shit,' Alyssa said. 'Did everybody just hear that?'

They turned. Although the immediate area above the pool was mired in darkness, subtle color began to peep through. First a wedge of grey, as if the windows on the other side had simply been blotted out, then different sections began to take shape.

It's not taking shape, Carolina thought. *It's growing.*

The wail grew even louder, and by its din rose a shape misshapen but angular, its sides perforated with bulging protuberances like parasites stuck to its hide. Though over two decades had passed since she'd last seen the cloud underwater, little had changed now it had arrived again. A black dervish, a riotous mass of form, puffing out a wake of energy like a coronal ejection.

Candles were dropped and flashlights lit once more.

One by one, they focused on the apparition as it drifted slowly toward them.

'Jason,' Alyssa said. 'Why did you have to ask that question?'

With Dillion filming again they backed up into the aisle, no one asserting which direction they should take or what moved toward them. Carolina, though lacking a writer's vocabulary, had done more than an adequate job describing her attacker. *You've come home, Carolina*, the cloud seemed to say as it drifted closer. *Come home to Daddy.*

Two at a time they navigated the stairs, Carolina resisting the temptation to take small peeks above or risk colliding into Jason ahead. Reaching the bottom tier, they built into a sprint past the conference rooms, through the labyrinthine turnstiles, then into the main foyer. The thing's wail, which Carolina had likened to a loon, suddenly changed in pitch – a foghorn-howl like something being denied.

Before reaching the glass doors, Dillion turned around and came to a complete stop, simple curiosity seeming to take over. So did Jeff. Then Jason. Soon they had all come to a standstill, staring up at a thing that had no right to existence in an ordinary world. Grown even larger, it loomed above them like a deity brought to life, the many facets of its hide now displaying faces contorted in the throes of some nameless appetite.

While Dillion kept his camera trained above, Carolina reached out and tugged his arm, fretful they could soon succumb to the same fugue state she'd fell victim to as a young girl. He seemed to get the message, at least partially.

Exiting the building, he kept his iPhone pointed at the cloud, now grown disproportionally to the size of a swimming pool itself and moving in for the kill.

SEVEN

It was Jeff's idea to hunker down in a small office for a while.

'I cleaned this particular room myself the whole time I was here,' he said as Dillion jimmied the lock. Loose and rusted, it came apart easily. 'Never felt a thing. Not so much as a bad vibe.'

Though Jason now had the overwhelming urge to leave, he understood the logic to sit still for a spell and get their bearings. The screaming had been one thing, the dog another. But staring up at a black manifestation straight from the bowels of a different world – a world they had been discussing in able tones directly before it emerged – was enough to bruise the sturdiest mind. His belief system, which up until now made room for all kinds of miracles, simply refused to grasp what the cloud had represented.

Something evil. Something with appetite.

Inwardly he prayed (as much as he could with these strangers present) but the words felt hollow, the entreaties meaningless. God, that stalwart of sanity his entire life, had not deigned to accompany Jason in tonight's quest. Upon stepping into the building, his presence had seemingly retracted altogether ... as if Providence Place was simply beyond God's measure of understanding.

'God,' he muttered. 'Has left the building.'

The others stared at him – and by their expressions Jason realized he'd spoken out loud. Shrugging in return, he looked away.

Though a few office chairs lay scattered around the small room, Jason's back once again found a wall. Flashlight beams, still the only form of adequate lighting, made cell-like patterns on the walls and ceiling.

'Jason's right,' Alyssa said. 'I vote we leave.'

Dillion's camera had disappeared for the moment. He said, 'Jason didn't say anything about leaving.'

'But that's what you meant, right? God has certainly left the fucking building. And in his place, Carolina's demon is chasing us around the school. Dillion, you have more than enough evidence on that puny little camera of yours. Let's get out of here while the getting's good.'

'Oh, no you don't,' said Carolina. Sweat clung to her face in beaded rivulets. 'You can't weasel out now, Alyssa. Not without facing your own shitty demons. That's not fair.'

'Fair? I thought *you* of all people would understand. How can you want to stay after what we all just saw? How –'

'Quiet!' Jeff shouted. 'All of you. Let's not fall into the bickering trap.'

After a sustained silence, Jason said, 'He's right.'

That's what happens in all those dumb ghost shows –
everybody starts arguing and things fall apart. Alyssa –
your experience was in the theater. Let's just go there and
get it over and done with. Then we leave.'

'But that *thing* –'

'Is probably contained in the swimming center,'
Carolina said. 'That's the feeling I got from it. Like that's
its territory.'

Jason could see Alyssa struggling. *Carolina's right.
She's not scared of the cloud at all. She's trying to avoid
going into the theater.*

Briefly his own sordid memories of Father
Parrington's last sermon came flooding back: Father
Parrington stumbling down the altar steps, his blistered,
varicose hands held out like a supplicant to his own
congregation. Gifford's head drooped down in an obscene
parody of Christ's lament, his dead and unfocused eyes
fixed on the blood congealed carpet below.

Who can blame her, he thought. *Dear God, please give
us strength.*

Again there was no answer from God, only the
director's assured voice cutting through the murk.

'One story to go,' he said. 'Then we get out of here.'

Above, cloud cover obscured the stars; a grey morass
of billowed forms whose lower portions scraped the higher
rooftops. Walking through another quadrangle of basketball
courts, Jason discerned the theater building as a black pile
of featureless brick. When they were close enough to see
the doors, something else emerged from the mist.

'You've gotta be fucking *kidding* me,' Alyssa said. 'A lone swing-set? The only thing missing with this picture is ominous music.'

While Dillion filmed the swings, the others circumnavigated the shot. Perhaps predictably, Alyssa stopped well short before they reached the doors. Looking over at Jason as he passed, she hugged her thin frame and gave him a listless look.

She whispered, 'I don't want to do this.'

And all at once Jason felt sorry for her. Here was the real Alyssa, bereft of any mask. Everything she wore to cover it: the sarcasm, the thinly veiled hostility – all of it was just a smokescreen for this vulnerable creature. Though she may have carried a chip on her shoulder as a kid, the things in her past here, whatever they might be, had been a catalyst fire to mold the woman.

Reassuringly, he tried to smile. But it felt bogus. So he reached out and placed a hand on her shoulder, guiding her last few steps until they reached the others.

'This one is locked too,' said Jeff. 'Dillion, we're probably going to need that crowbar again.'

A small battle ensued while the door was manhandled, both men taking turns in the effort. A grunt of success came from Jeff when it finally broke loose.

As they walked into the theater, no screams could be heard through the mist.

And no dark cloud followed them from above.

On the inside, posters from a different era greeted them. Encased in dust-smeared glass display cases, the pictures featured both cinema and Broadway advertisements. In what was a grim echo of the classrooms, the small foyer had all the trappings of a time capsule … or perhaps a town abandoned by nuclear fallout. The film posters sported titles such as *Batman Returns* and Kevin Costner's *The Bodyguard*; Broadway: *The Blues Brothers Show* and *Anna Karenina*. Here was a testament not only to the early nineties, but to a pocket of the school where the real world was put on hold and the imagination given reign. Among the Hollywood memorabilia: framed photos of the high-school kids in action, donning everything from wigs to make-up in an attempt to satirize the tragic, the comedic, and everything in between. Jeff's world had been dirty; Alyssa's just the opposite: a glamourous parade of the mind. Beneath the framed posters Jason spied a pile of banners, now streaked with muddy footprints, cobbled together by students handy with a pen.

'*Fiddler on the Roof*,' Jason said, and bent down to expose the others. '*Lord of the Flies*. Gosh, I think every school in the country still does that one.'

Alyssa, eyeing the pictures with wonder, appeared to have forgotten her fear. 'Would you look at this,' she said, skating her fingers over the dust of a framed photograph. 'I remember the day this was taken. During rehearsals for *Macbeth*.'

They leaned in, Dillion already lapping up production value. Featuring about fifteen students, Alyssa's smiling visage toward the back was unmistakable. Streaked blonde hair and the physique of a cheerleader. Eyes that emitted light. She'd been radiant, the smiling apogee of every girl-next-door type Jason had been terrified of approaching in high school. Sensing something (perhaps a list of dreams never realized), Alyssa's smile suddenly waned.

'She was sixteen when production of *The Hanging* began,' Dillion blurted, speaking into his cell but keeping it pointed at the picture. 'Sarah Knowles, head of the drama department, offered Alyssa the role without an audition. A controversial play penned by one of the seniors of the school's aspiring playwrights, Sean Hoare, *The Hanging* was widely criticized by the school board and concerned parents alike for its macabre subject matter and taboo sex scenes.'

Alyssa turned around, began to move away.

'Jesus,' Carolina said. 'Could you regulate that inane chatter of yours to the background? The girl is standing right here in front of you.'

But Dillion had found his moment – perhaps one he'd been planning in advance. 'From day one, actress Alyssa Asterious would champion the play, becoming a poster child for a production that would feature acts of witchcraft, torture, and even titular incest taking place during the seventeenth century. The local press, always on the lookout where Providence Place was concerned, followed the controversy closely. In the lead up to *The Hanging*'s premiere, after-hours debates often took place within the school, these involving everyone from parents to freedom of speech activists who would travel over from Brown University.'

Alyssa had wandered away from them further, over toward the stage doors as if lost. For a minute she stood still, one hand clamped over her mouth. Then, in the same dream-like manner, she reached forward and pushed open the right-hand door.

'In the end, nothing could stop the play from going ahead,' Dillion continued, this time with no intervention from his cast. '*The Hanging* would have its premiere, mostly thanks to the tireless work of its lead actress.'

Years of inaction saw the theater door produce an awkward, complaining dirge. Though Jason almost called out (not wanting Alyssa to go in alone) he couldn't quite bring himself to do it. He wanted to see her reaction. He wanted to observe just as Dillion's camera observed.

Without stopping to lift her torch, Alyssa stepped forward and disappeared into the dark.

Gone forever, Jason's mind whispered. *The school just swallowed her up.*

But of course their torches revealed no such oddity as they all proceeded through. While the dark was indeed deep, Alyssa could still be discerned as a moving outline forging ahead. Now coming into play: Jason's memory from the few times he had actually spent in this building. Never one to cotton onto the acting side of things, his brief visits to the theater had been spent as an audience member, more often than not being dragged here by his mother when plays of the religious ilk were being performed. He remembered another small anteroom … and then the beginnings of the audience seating: red chairs raised in the same ascending manner of a church pew. In between, before the stage itself, was a bizarre no-man's land encompassing perhaps twenty feet of black linoleum – a mote separating the action from the audience. Sometimes, when bored teachers' curriculums were found wanting, Jason recalled them bustling their students in during rehearsals. He *distinctly* recalled food being launched from the seats if said students found rehearsals displeasing.

Traversing the mote, each flashlight beam illuminated debris that was now all too familiar: the severed heads of broken dolls; the somehow forlorn presence of a single boot. What stood out more than any physical item was the clinging smell seemingly pertinent to all theaters: a cozy aroma of chair padding and popcorn. And underneath all that: the subtle whiff of papier-mâché, building blocks for stage props.

The world of the theater bloomed into light – all of it: the mote, audience seating, and even the stage itself snapping into focus as if a switch had been thrown. Which of course it had. Dillion, idling back, had found the main switchboard housing every light known to man.

'Jesus *Christ*,' Jeff snapped.

Carolina said, 'You could have freaking *warned* us.'

Ignoring them completely, Dillion made haste for the stage.

He looks, Jason thought, *like a man who knows something we don't. A man with an ace up his sleeve.* And all at once Kristen's face surfaced in his mind's eye; Kristen shrill and accusatory. *You chose a strange man's project over my advice to stay away from Providence Place? How could you do that, Jason? How could you choose between an idiot director and the only girl who's ever gone to bed with you?*

He thought of telling her that by undertaking this pilgrimage, he was committing to an act whereby his nightmares of Father Parrington could potentially cease. But there was no point. Kristen's voice, in addition to her visage, was becoming as indoctrinated into his thoughts and actions as his late mother's.

Switching off his flashlight, Jason looked toward the stage platform. Beside one object, it was entirely empty ... and it was the last thing he would have expected to see remaining behind. Or was it? Now that he was staring at it, perhaps it was the *only* thing.

The gallows were set back about ten feet from the edge of the raised platform, a triangular wooden edifice with three uprights and three cross beams; ropes were still attached to the center beam. Observing the execution device, he didn't need to ask Alyssa or anybody else if this particular gallows had been used for *The Hanging* stage play. Nor did he have to wonder what came next.

'*The Hanging* featured a series of explicit executions,' Dillion piped into his phone. 'Not explicit in the act themselves – plays like Shakespeare's are, after all, steeped in blood. No, what made these ones a form of contention among the faculty were having children at the mercy of the gallows, teenagers for the most part, who were strung up for crimes pertaining to lascivious acts in the fictitious world the author had presented in *The Hanging*.'

This was Alyssa's story being told, Jason realized. But told with a different kind of theatrics. Gone were the evenly spaced stuttering candles; gone too an ushering into the narrative. Instead there was an addled girl who was having her tale belligerently thrust upon her. Still exuding that trance-like state, Alyssa walked to the small wooden block that would see her take the stage. Her expression (the look of a woman who sees an accident and can't look away) was reserved wholly for the gallows and the three pieces of rope fostered to the center beam.

Treading softly, Dillion loitered behind her. He said, 'Spread by word of mouth, *The Hanging* played to packed audiences two, sometimes three times in a week – unheard of at the time for a play penned by one of the students. Already an established drawcard for those seeking the mysterious or the occult, the play's subject matter and Alyssa's performance all added to the circus that was Providence Place. It was during one of these runs when things went horribly wrong for one member of the cast.'

Having reached the stage, Alyssa proceeded to walk to the gallows, never once diverting her gaze. Jason looked at the others, expecting one of them to chime in. But Jeff and Carolina also appeared strung-out, their listless stares following Alyssa's trajectory as if they were audience members waiting for some kind of punchline.

'Sadie Whitmore was only thirteen years of age during *The Hanging's* run,' Dillion said. 'She would have been fourteen in November of that year. Besides drama, she liked badminton and her fellow students remember her as a fine drawer who often joked about going into the tattoo business. Sadie played the character of Elise Wilmus, a protestant of the new world who would be put on trial for crimes of witchcraft and ultimately executed. Her character's death took place in the third act during the climax of the narrative. Though a thin noose was placed around the neck of all the condemned before the floor gave way beneath them, a small Velcro clasp ensured it came undone. Not exactly standard practice as an effect, but if the actor kept their chin firmly wedged to their neck, it was often visually effective. On the night of the twenty-third of

September, with the entire cast and a few hundred audience members looking on expectantly, Sadie Whitmore had a real noose secured around her neck before her sentence was carried out. When the bottom gave way underneath, she began choking to death.'

Now facing the nooses, Alyssa reached out a hand and touched the one closest to her. She began to caress it ... then lifted the lower portion toward her face. That broke Jason's paralysis, and he called out her name. Of course, he had no real idea what her motivation was, but that didn't warrant some kind of intrusion here. Dillion's monotone drawl had her in a state akin to sleepwalking. Like a pied-piper of gallows humor.

Deigning not even a blink, Alyssa ignored him.

Dillion had now reached the stage. He said, 'Giddy moments went by when the audience assumed it was all part of the performance, of course. A common occurrence during all kinds of real life tragedies. People simply refuse to believe the tragedy is real. Clearly seen on the two cameras that filmed it, and according to eye-witness police reports, Sadie's feet kicked and her eyes bulged. Still no one moved. Then, the front of her dress flowered with urine. Still jerking, her movements were convulsive enough to finally tear the noose free from its moorings. Then she spilled onto the floorboards. With the first screams came the first responders from the sides, while some of the front row audience also rushed the platform. But it's all too late. Sadie's trachea had undergone the blunt force of major trauma. Despite efforts to revive her, Sadie Whitmore was dead.'

Dillion stood close to Alyssa, his breath only inches

from her neck. Oblivious, Alyssa stopped caressing the noose and made a languid effort to place it over her head. Then all at once everybody was calling her name, Jeff breaking his own fugue state and galloping up the wooden balustrade in massive strides. At the sound of his feet, Jason noticed Alyssa's eyes clear all at once, and she turned around to stare at their director as if just awakening. 'I'm sorry,' she said, and Jason was relieved to see a glint of her old mischievousness return. 'I don't know what came over me.'

Despite his small stature, Jeff casually manhandled Dillion aside. For the moment, his narration had ceased.

'The dressing rooms,' Alyssa said. Having discarded the noose, she peered at her would-be rescuer with a new-found zeal. 'I told Dillion I wouldn't go in there … that I *couldn't*. Oh, God. Sadie. She came to me afterward – came to see me in the dressing rooms.'

Jeff placed a hand on her back and motioned her to the left, guiding her away from the gallows. Alyssa went obligingly enough, now staring at the spot where a girl name Sadie Whitmore had breathed her last.

'The dressing rooms are through here, down the corridor,' said Dillion.

His strange look of appetite never waned.

Away from the gallows, Jason felt better already. Just being in its general proximity had instilled a feeling of dread. Backstage, they traversed a thin corridor painted a bilious green.

'I don't remember hearing about Sadie at all,' Carolina

said. 'What happened? Was it just an accident? Or was she … set up to fall?'

'I've got a better question,' Jeff said. 'What are the gallows still *doing* in here? Why weren't they removed?'

'They were removed,' Alyssa replied absently.

No one responded. But Jason knew what they were all thinking. *Providence Place brought them back. Returned the gallows just special for the returning pilgrims.*

A ridiculous notion. But was it anymore ridiculous than a wraithlike dog or a writhing cloud of faces? For the first time, Jason reflected on everything they had witnessed thus far, everything that Dillion had bottled away. What would happen when this was all over? Would they all become famous, as their director had obviously envisioned? Or would they be ridiculed and mocked, loathed as clever hoaxers and regulated to the shadows? It probably happened all the time, even to genuine cases.

Will you even survive the night? a voice (Kristen's again) whispered, and Jason tuned it down before it could say anything else.

With still no need for their flashlights (banks of bulbs were lit up everywhere) the end of the corridor came into view. Surrounding it like watchmen were two doors. One on the left, and one on the right. Both of them inscribed with something. Alyssa, second in the marching parade, slowed to a crawl. Then she stopped completely. Jason didn't need to look at her eyes to ascertain they would be bugging out again.

'Alyssa,' Carolina said. 'I take back what I said before. You don't have to do this. It doesn't matter what you signed. *Screw* what you signed. If you don't want to go inside those dressing rooms, you don't have to.'

Hearing the voice of her one-time victim (a voice now riddled with a species of compassion) seemed to waylay any impending regression. Dropping her hand, Alyssa looked at each of them in turn, even managing to tip Jason a small smile. He smiled back. Perhaps the soldiers of the world were right, after all. Perhaps calamity, even of the otherworldly kind, really did strengthen bonds.

'It's like Jason said. I know I don't have to, but unless I do, a part of me will be always here, coming in to audition every day. Another part will be hearing Sadie drop to the gallows floor like a sack of cement. And yet another part …' Her eyes moved toward the door on the left. 'Let's just get *this* part over with, then we can all get the fuck out of here.'

'Amen,' Jason said.

Having already moved ahead, Dillion tested the strength of the left door. Satisfied, he teased it open, all the while filming and groping on the other side for a light switch. Now close enough to discern the type, Jason was pleased to discover it was nothing more arbitrary than *GIRLS* written in black and embossed with glitter. The one on the right proclaimed *BOYS*, and there wasn't a smattering of graffiti – lewd or otherwise – to be seen.

'Sadie Whitmore's death was eventually ruled an accident,' Dillion mumbled into his palm, pushing his way into the now well-lit room. 'Although an attempt was made by her parents to be compensated for neglect. It would be *The Hanging*'s last performance, of course, with its detractors getting the final say and some opining the theater should be bulldozed into the ground. They wanted the site as a memorial for Sadie. Eventually, the school board would cave partly to the request, though it seemed the theater had one final show to perform.'

With the door ajar they filed in, and the first thing to jump out at Jason was his own reflection staring back. Mirrors, some of them large enough to run from floor to ceiling, flanked an entire room bereft of any windows. Chairs, desks, and even make-up products sat in front of these. Not for the first time, Jason was reminded of Chernobyl, a metropolis whose citizens had evacuated at the drop of a hat. Here, the same kind of tableaus were in evidence. There were wigs still attached to dummies; there were costumes adorning them. In addition to the splayed bags of makeup, Jason spied what could only be the remnants of a half-finished doughnut, its once glazed face encrusted with dust. Dozens of additional posters plastered wall-space that wasn't gilded with a mirror. Some, he saw, were even advertisements for *The Hanging* itself.

From his left, the sound of small sobs. The star of *The Hanging* had also found the posters.

Dillion said, 'Tell us what happened to you in here, Alyssa. Tell us what you saw.'

Mascara running freely down both cheeks, Alyssa walked over to the closest mirror. She reached out and absently cut a streak through almost two decades of accumulated dust.

'Carolina's right,' said Jeff. 'You don't have to say anything.'

Perhaps for the first time this night, Dillion lowered his phone. *He* didn't say anything, merely kept an accusatory stare trained on Jeff. Then, with no retort coming from the former janitor, he lifted it up again. Instead of homing in on Alyssa this time, he trained it on her reflection.

'There isn't really much to the story at all,' Alyssa said. 'You guys probably have me beat in the entertainment department. One Friday night after school I came in here by myself. Nothing was in production, of course – and nothing would be ever again. I'm not really sure what compelled me to come in that night. To say goodbye, I suppose. This was once a magical place for me. For everyone who worked in drama. But they were going to tear it down. I sat right there, in that seat, for God-knows how long. At least until I started to nod off a little, anyway. When I came to, I had no idea what time it was or how long I had been napping for. Cell phones were still a thing of the future. When I got up to leave, I discovered the door had been locked shut.'

Jason looked at said door … and noticed something he hadn't before – something besides the word *GIRLS* all glittered up. Underneath the doorknob was a wide array of dirty markings and indentations. The kind produced by fingernails, perhaps. A sudden queasy feeling began to unfurl in his stomach.

'I called out but knew it wasn't going to do any good. Everyone in the quadrant outside had packed up and left for the weekend. And there was nobody in the building besides me.'

Jeff was also staring at her reflection when he spoke. 'You didn't think someone on the other side might have locked you in?'

The reflection shook its head. 'No, I didn't. Strangely enough, the thought didn't really enter my head. I just …

knew it was something else.'

Again Jason wanted to scream. *Why doesn't anyone just say it this time? The unseen world* ...

'I didn't panic at first, just checked the room for something that might help me. Looked for nail files to pick the lock or maybe a hidden grate to crawl through.' Wiping away more dust with side of her palm, Alyssa barked out a short cackle. 'As you can see there aren't any.

'Then I did the typical things – started banging on the door and pushing my weight against it. Then I started hollering. After a while I guess I started to scream a little. Not long after that, the lights went out for the first time, and when they did, I knew I wasn't the only one standing in the girls' dressing room.'

Alyssa turned around and faced the camera. Jason noted her odd disjointed look had returned. 'Because I could hear her breathing, you see. Sadie, I could hear her.'

Impeccable delivery, Kristen's ghost voice whispered. *Don't forget she's still an actress.*

'Even then I didn't totally lose it – just tried to keep calm as the breathing became louder and heavier and closer. Finally, when it was close enough to reach out and touch me, I *did* lose it. Screamed like a girl who was auditioning for a slasher role. By the time I was done my voice was hoarse. Then the lights came back on.'

Dillion said, 'This continued, didn't it Alyssa? The lights kept going off and on like somebody was flicking a breaker switch?'

Alyssa nodded. For a brief second, her eyes found the floor. 'I was down there, in a fetal position with my back against the wall. The lights came on for about three minutes, then went dark for about five. And each time, I could hear the breathing getting louder and louder. I think she was ... using the dark somehow, you know? Using it like stepping through a window. Somehow it was making her stronger. Finally she appeared.'

Jason stared at the floor. It was hard not to picture the entire room as a kind of memorial to time; all of it bulging with infamy. All across the globe, houses continued to stand where momentous things had transpired – places like the mansion where Sharon Tate and her offspring were butchered; places like the Amityville house in Long Island where a family was murdered and ghosts purportedly reigned. Despite their history, people still walked around that very air as if the events themselves had never occurred. Yet Jason had little doubt they felt *something*. Because he was feeling it right now. As if the present moment was fragile and history itself was attempting to break through.

'It was like all the horror movies I'd ever seen. At first she didn't appear in the room, only in the mirror. And the time when the lights went out until they came back on got shorter and shorter. When they came back on, it was just like the breathing. She kept creeping closer and closer. I could see her hair, black like floating kelp or seaweed. Then her face. The movies have one thing right, and that's that ghosts mostly keep the form they die in. Sadie's left eye hung partway over her cheek, bulging. Her skin was a web work of purple veins crisscrossing each other. Her forehead was *black*. She wasn't quite standing, wasn't quite crawling. Just *slinking* toward me. And her right eye worked perfectly, let me tell you that. What I saw in that one eye ... she was mad. She was angry at me for letting her die.'

When Alyssa lifted her arm this time, Jason saw the hand attached shaking. She held it out toward the camera as if beseeching Dillion – or just trying to make him understand her plight. 'I screamed and I pleaded with her, said it wasn't my fault. But of course it was, wasn't it? It was *all* our faults. Sure, we may not have set up the gallows to literally hang her, but we were culpable for not really *giving a shit*. I know I didn't. Do you know what the first thing to come into my mind was when the ambulance showed up? That it would be good publicity for the play. That it would be good for *me*. That this tragedy would finally get me noticed, and I could ship out to Hollywood post haste and finally get away from this shitty town and even shittier school with its never-ending parade of misfortunes.'

She paused, now breathing in ragged gulps. Though Dillion's expression foretold he wanted to say something, for the moment his trap was shut. So was Jeff's. Carolina was also looking at the floor, her cheeks screwed up as if she were in the process of swallowing something unpleasant.

'But everyone knows nothing like that happened. If there's one thing teenagers do well, it's overachieving in the art of self-delusion. No one came calling to whisk me away to greener pastures, no one except Sadie, that is. I knew, seeing her, that she wanted me to join her. She wanted me to suffer on the other side. Although not straight away, either, no siree. I had a very long weekend to look forward to.'

The next part Jason was somewhat familiar with. The

aftermath of her ordeal, anyway. No mention of ghosts in the newspaper articles – just a story about a girl who had been trapped in one of the buildings for a few days before anybody raised the alarm. And Jason thought he even knew the reason why that was. Though it was possible she may have been close to her parents, Alyssa Asterious had carried a reputation. One of late nights and loose antics. Taking off for a few days at a time on a weekend without notifying anyone wouldn't have been all that uncommon … not for a girl who was chauffeured around the area by boys who played on the football team. Like Alyssa had stated, this was the era before Facebook updates. None of her close friends would have had any means of monitoring her absence.

Her eyes had moved back to the mirror. 'Anybody read that book *Cujo*? Seen the movie? Strangely it was that stupid story my mind kept circling around to as I lay huddled here. I was trapped in a theater … but I may as well have been trapped in a busted Pinto with a rabid dog circling me. That first night, the lights eventually came back on for a long time, and I somehow managed to fall asleep. I had to go to the bathroom, of course, and after filling up an empty cup I found in the trash I started going in the corner. And I was thirsty, too. So thirsty I can't even describe it. When I awoke, I could hear faint birdsong outside so I knew it was morning. I kept hoping someone playing sports across the road would hear my screams. Or maybe just some of the maintenance people. Then Sadie came back.'

Dillion had moved closer so his viewfinder was within eyeshot. Through the screen, Jason could see Alyssa's

Adam's-apple filling the frame and bobbing up and down as she swallowed … as though she were recalling her long ago thirst. Or perhaps what her pee had tasted like. Which wasn't outside the realm of possibility. Though, of course, she wouldn't admit to such a thing. Which was a welcome relief after everything –

'I'd read about Poltergeists,' Alyssa said. 'Who hasn't? Who hasn't seen *that* movie? A malevolent force able to access the physical world we live in. Able to pick stuff up and throw shit around. But it was *me* being thrown around. I felt my hair being pulled when it went dark – pulled out by the root on some occasions. I felt my face being slapped. I could hear whispering too, so loud it seemed to go up into my ear canal. And do you know the things it said? That I was a *cunt*. That I was a slut. That I was a no-good fucking whore who should be strung up by a rope for *existing*. By late afternoon, what I assumed was afternoon, I was pacing around like an animal in a cage. And then the mirrors started to come alive.'

'You started hallucinating?' Carolina asked, speaking up for the first time in a while. Her voice was tinny with dread.

Alyssa flashed her eyes toward her. 'It wasn't just Sadie I saw staring back at me, there were … others. People I didn't recognize. Small children for the most part. They promised me relief – said that if I walked into the mirror and joined them I could escape the bad girl tormenting me. Because *she* was trapped in here, in the theater. Part of me knew I was probably experiencing the onset of cabin fever … or even, yes, hallucinating. But another part knew of me knew better. These children, some of them wore the school uniform. Others were garbed in get-up from last century. I swear I even recognized one – Stacy Marshall who'd died of Leukemia when I was in fourth grade. They whispered, they cajoled, but I knew it wasn't really them so I didn't listen. I knew if I walked up to that mirror, if I walked *through* it, then I really would join the bitch who was haunting me.'

Stacy Marshall who had died of Leukemia in fourth grade …

Though Jason didn't remember any Stacy, what Alyssa had just said carried more dark weight than anything thus far. Taking into account her disease, the girl would have died far away from Providence Place; in all likelihood she would have died in a hospital surrounded by her parents and loved ones. To consider the possibility, however remote, that a soul educated here eventually returned here like a bird to its nesting grounds was something Jason wouldn't contemplate. *Couldn't.* Such a thing was anathema to his entire belief system.

Why not? Kristen remarked. *You've never seen any evidence for your own God whatsoever. But you've seen plenty of evidence for life after death. And it's all taken place right here in Providence Place. Glenn Frey knew what he was singing about there, don't you think? You can check out anytime you like, hon, but you can never leave.*

Alyssa said, 'Not a very nice thought, is it? Spending eternity in *this* place.' She hiccuped a laugh, and Jason came to the sudden realization she hadn't sparked a single cigarette since they had entered the building.

'My second night was even worse, but by that stage I'd convinced myself I had the fortitude to see things through until Monday. My little prison stank, too. Holy God did it stink. This blue carpet here is new. After I escaped, they had the old one uprooted and replaced. Like they do in houses if a cat or a dog pisses too much on the floor over the span of its life. So I slept and I pissed, pissed and then slept some more. When I woke, there were purple bruises on my face and calves. When I looked into the mirror, I saw myself on the end of a rope, swaying by its tether. Sometimes the children called my name; sometimes they came right up to my side. But I held on, somehow I held on. On Sunday night, just over forty-eight hours after becoming locked in, one of the music teachers came by spur-of-the-moment to pick up a guitar he'd accidently left over the weekend. I didn't hear him, though. He heard me. Heard my crying. When he opened the door, he claimed it wasn't locked. Can you believe that? What he saw when he walked in probably has him going to a therapist for life.'

And there it was: Alyssa's eventual rescue after two days of being locked in a theater dressing room. Dehydrated and carrying substantial bruises, she was otherwise physically fine. After her mother had picked her up (the woman and Principal Hague exchanging fierce entreaties that had included threats from both parties), Alyssa had gone home to stand in her shower stall for over two hours. Both her mother and father had concluded the bruises to be self-inflicted, despite evidence to the contrary. On Monday morning, now clean but only speaking in muted whispers, Alyssa had made clear her intentions of parting ways with Providence Place. There would be no returning to the school that had made her a local star; there would be no tearful farewells to teachers and student friends she had spent her childhood and adolescence accruing.

'I ended up coming clean for the same reason you did, Carolina,' Alyssa said. 'I needed tuition money for college. So two years later, I approached the trashiest of trashiest – that piece of shit magazine known as *The Star*. They put me on the front page and did an expose featuring mostly bullshit, stuff that jived more with Carolina's story and made their headline more of a sensationalist scream. Then I got on with my life and tried to forget it ever happened.'

Now, finally, a cigarette was lit. With both smoke and voice trembling, Alyssa said, 'Until Dillion, that was. Until Dillion-fucking-Cook here called me out-of-the-blue three weeks ago and offered me the returning role for a sequel.'

EIGHT

Exiting through a backdoor, the five made their way across a small overgrown carpark before coming to another set of buildings for sports equipment storage. Beyond these rose the back fence, a serrated enclosure that would not be out of place in a prison. Past the fence were the ovals of Providence Place, three conjoined football fields where every sport imaginable had once played host. During his early researches, Dillion had scoured hundreds of photos of the area in its prime. Looking at it now, it was easy to believe they were two separate environments, as completely disparate from each other as the surface of the moon and the innards of a forest. The grass, neglected for over a decade now, was more in keeping with an everglade swamp. Everywhere hung the smell of bore water, a metallic miasma like freshly pumped sewage.

It was Jeff who noticed the second school bus.

'I'll be damned,' was all Dillion heard the man say. Then he was away at a trot, trench coat flapping behind him like an ill-fitting cape.

Like most things seen on this night, Dillion's shaky-cam found the bus before his eyes. Following Jeff, its dirty side was as visible as a yellow smudge against the night. Behind him, his three other subjects quickly caught up, Alyssa giving voice to some trademark expletives.

Should've pushed her further back there, he thought. *In the end she didn't give me what I needed: a complete submission to her fears. None of them did. There's still time, though. Still lots of time to get that final –*

'Wait!' Jeff called from up ahead. He had come to a standstill ten feet from the front of the bus, one hand held up high. He did not turn around as Dillion approached.

'What is it now?' Dillion asked. Despite the darkness, an ominous (and entirely concealed) light source seemed to sketch out the scene in stark relief; Dillion could see the bus's front bumper and headlights as if they were superimposed on a projectionist's screen. Surrounding the vehicle was all manner of detritus – newspapers, beer bottles, and even food packaging. To the left, the black outline of what appeared to be a couch.

'Shhh,' Jeff whispered, bringing down his hand to touch his lips. Never breaking eye contact with the bus for a second, he said, 'Tell the others to hush when they get here.'

But there was no need to tell them anything. Advancing lightly as though on a tightrope, Dillion filmed them purveying the trash, then swung his camera back to the bus.

'There's a small fire back there,' said Jeff. He took two steps forward, paused, then reached down and gingerly unsheathed his gun. As he began moving again, Dillion followed closely behind like a shadow.

Just what does a small fire mean?

That you're not alone, of course, a voice whispered in reply. *And you never were. Who do you think arranged all those mannequins in the children's library? Who do you think authored the graffiti? Someone, or something, is living in the school – someone a lot more interesting than any homeless stew bum or nightmare animal ...*

Past the bus's one open door now, and the evidence for this was mounting. Leading up to the driver's seat were three steps, each of them festooned with more food items: empty candy wrappers and milk cartons – production value if Dillion had ever seen it. Although they had passed a lot of similar refuse on this sojourn, some of this stuff appeared fresh, the hoarding remnants of a hermit. For a moment he was assailed by an image, horrid in its simplicity: Sadie Whitmore living on in this abandoned bus. She would still have her rope, of course, and unresolved business with a leading lady ...

In front of Jeff came a sound: the snap and crackle of burning. It was a fire, all right. And it lay just out of sight beyond the barrel end of the bus. Smoke plumes eddied over the roof and disappeared into the sky.

Jeff turned around. 'Stay here. I'll go up ahead first.'

Jason whispered, 'Shouldn't we check inside the bus first?'

Jeff's head shook in the negative, pointed to his gun as if that was all the reasoning he needed. 'Just stay here,' he said.

More rubbish lay piled underneath the vehicle, Dillion

saw; the flotsam and jetsam of a parade. Angling his
camera down, the iPhone's meager light illuminated a
banner bearing Providence Place's many totems: the lion
and the scroll. Underneath these an open book and the front
façades glaring windows and obelisk turrets. He bent down,
trying to see in further, and felt a hand cup him from
behind. He was about to shrug it off when footsteps began
at the back of the bus.

Footsteps.

The group froze, animals in headlights. The footsteps
(*oh yes that's footsteps, all right. Boots, if I'm not
mistaken*)
reverberated off the bottom of the cab and seemed to
travel through the spine of the bus before settling into the
windows. Now they were in the middle. Now gaining
steadily toward the front. Dillion peered upward through
dark glass and could see nothing but a carnival reflection of
their own bulbous heads. Ahead, Jeff had swiveled back
around, his gun pointed directly into the maw of Dillion's
camera.

Whoever the footsteps belonged to stopped at the apex,
presumably in the cab, next to the driver's seat. Ignoring
the gun, Dillion trained his view-finder on his mismatched
cast, each one of them now trained in a rigid stance.
About to call out, the owner of the boots saved him the
trouble by traversing the last few strides and stepping out
into the smoke-addled night.

Standing around six-foot-two, a long-haired denizen
sporting a black trench coat held a sawed-off shotgun in
both palms. The amber glow of a cigarette floated in the
shadow of his face. With his entrance had also come his

smell … a scent, Dillion now realized, that seemed to embody the school itself: purple chewing gum and molding attics; the earthen, somehow sweet aroma of crushed leaves left to rot.

For a second the moment stretched, a stand-off punctuated by silence. Then the man spoke, 'You, put down your weapon.'

Behind Dillion Jeff didn't hesitate. There came a metallic thump as he lowered his pistol.

He sees your camera. Now would probably be a good time to lower it, too.

But doing so somehow went against the grain of everything Dillion knew. Events didn't happen unless they were documented. That was the awful truth of the modern world. He had been counting on a surprise twist, and now a pun called providence had shown him the way. Here stood the fifth business and change agent; a joker in the deck to herald in the McGuffin. Instead of dropping the camera, Dillion palmed the zoom button.

Inside the viewfinder, Jeff's gun had been replaced by an even bigger one.

The stranger looked closely at them, reserving his core attention for Carolina. Then he lowered the butt of his shotgun.

'Mom,' the vagrant said. 'You've finally come home.'

It was the kind of reveal Dillion could not have foreseen even if the night had been scripted. Certainly not the kind reserved for a category of film belonging in the found-footage niche. A prodigal son, born of a virgin, decides to return home to the place of his conception. A family reunion in the offing ... reunification of both mother and son set on the blasted landscape of a school. And where was Daddy in the equation? Why, he was everywhere, of course – he was in every lost corner and abandoned hallway. He was the black, malformed tide of a dark cloud. *The others don't get it; they haven't made the connection yet. And neither has Carolina.*

But slowly they did. Alyssa, her head moving from Carolina to the stranger, simply mouthed the words: *No.*

Then all at once Carolina's deportment changed; she seemed to shrivel inside herself. Taking a step closer, she peered at the newcomer as though addressing a familiar. Though no telltale features were evident, of course. In this light, there was no way to discern any physical similarities. But, as any twin or mother would no doubt know intuitively, sometimes parallels weren't needed.

Sometimes people just understood blood was thicker than water.

'Maddox?' she asked. And took another staggering step forward. '*Maddox?*'

Dillion filmed the stranger's Adam's-apple working as he rose to form a reply. Then he shifted his bodyweight and raised the shotgun again, suddenly taking aim at something to the left of the group.

An explosion of shotgun pellets rang out, the recoil like an avalanche of sound. Dillion ducked, cowering. Three shots later he slowly raised his head again.

Bent-backed and twisted, another strange animal had wandered into their midst, only to be cut down by the stranger. Far larger than Jeff's victim, its wounded flank grouted in blood. Bullets had gouged four ragged holes, each of them wide enough to display slick transparencies.

'They've started coming out at night,' the vagrant said matter-of-factly. Striding toward his kill, he moved like a man in need of a cane. 'There was a time they only moved during the day. Moved in packs, too, just like regular dogs. Back then they still *looked* like normal dogs. Enough so you could tell them apart, anyway.'

Bending over his considerable weight, the man grabbed the animal by its neck and hoisted it. A squelching sound could be heard as whatever made up the thing's anatomy went through its stealthy mode of decay. For a moment

(Maddox, dear God, is it really Maddox all grown up?)

the man did nothing but observe its rotating hindquarters. Then, with a noise of disgust, he flung it over his shoulder. It travelled in an overarching tailspin and landed among the abundant refuse. He turned back toward them.

'Look at you all,' said the vagrant. 'Don't you make a sight.'

'You knew I would be coming back?' Carolina asked.

The big man nodded slowly. 'Same as me, you see. After a while I didn't know where else to go. I never belonged out there in the real world. Up until the time you arrived just now, I had no idea it would be you. Then I saw you. And I knew.'

He paused, seemed to weigh this insight as if it held great fundamental truths. 'And I knew,' he repeated.

Somehow Dillion had secured both mother and son in the same shot, and for that brief moment, it was perfect.

Jeff, Alyssa, and Jason had faded to mere foreground actors; their stage presence no more tangible than the extras an audience sees but fails to register. The smoke continued to drift over, carrying with it soot-stained paper like black confetti, wafting around the actors as though manhandled by an unseen stage hand.

There.

This is what Dillion had tried and failed to bottle properly so far tonight: *pure production value.* Nothing had been quite as good as this; not even the dead woman on the riser, locked in her rigor-mortis scream. This was the porn of desolation but latticed with human emotion and given wings to fly. Whatever came next had to be –

'I knew you'd return, Momma,' said Maddox. He raised the weapon again. 'And now it's time for us to go home. It's what they want, you see.'

Dillion's still frame shattered; only to be replaced by the stark relief of reality: five strangers in a dungeon lair.

Arms open, Carolina took another step toward her son. 'What do you mean, Maddox?' she asked. 'Who are *they*?'

'I think you know, Momma,' Maddox said. 'Some nights when it's hard to sleep I can see them, moving over the school. Sometimes they talk to me, tell me what a good boy I've been for coming home. But it's not enough, you see. They want more. They want us to really come home.'

Despite Maddox's sudden proclamation, his gun lay inert. As the idiot insanity of the moment came to pass, Dillion's intellect tried to process and package it all up:

Maddox as a young boy put forth for adoption and moving in with a foster family; Maddox eventually finding

135

out, when coming of age, the true name of his birth mother, and in all probability not being surprised by the story surrounding her. Because Maddox was no ordinary child. If Carolina's story were to be fully believed, this vagrant standing in front of them was no doubt fitted with emotions and memories pertaining to another world ... to an unseen world – one where appetites and different states of being reigned supreme. The child, never feeling like it had belonged anywhere, had come back to its spawning ground as a young man; back to the place called Providence Place. And here he had waited, biding his time.

'Let's talk about this,' Carolina said, moving closer. She seemed stupefied, as if she'd just caught Dillion's internal revelations. 'I know we can talk about this.'

'Why'd you give me up, Momma?' said Maddox. *He's close to crying*, Dillion thought. 'Is it because you hate who I am? Is it because you hate *what I am*? I couldn't help being born, Momma. Any more than you could help what happened that morning when you went swimming in the pool.'

A sound on Dillion's immediate left. Jeff. He'd almost forgotten the man ... almost forgotten about his *gun*. The silhouettes of Jason and Alyssa were retreating. But he couldn't do the same, could he? Not now. Not when he finally had his money shot. Just a few more seconds and –

'I see things when I'm in the world, Momma. Horrible things. People are like *meat*, and I want to hurt them so bad. They tell me to hurt them. But not here. At least here it's quiet.'

In her right hand, Carolina now grasped one ample bosom. Her left made headway toward her son. She said,

'I'm so sorry I left, Maddox. But I couldn't provide you with a happy life. People have always been mean to me, so very mean. Even meaner after you were born. I know what it feels like … to not belong.'

Some of what Carolina said must have gotten through … at least a little. The rifle came down, and grown-up Maddox stared at his mother with the kind of look only an orphan could yield: confusion, abandonment, and unadulterated love all rolled into one.

Then the countenance cleared, and Carolina's son raised his shotgun for the final time.

NINE

Jeff looked on in muted horror as Carolina's torso blossomed black, then red, the interior of her guts spilling out. Only a foot or so from the blast, she was promptly flung backward, Jeff sidestepping her large frame at the last moment. Panicked, Alyssa and Jason bolted, their flashlight crossbeams like spotlights aimed at the sky. Before Jeff could do the same, he chanced a momentary look down at Carolina's body, its slumped contours already evincing lifelessness.

Her dead eyes stared past him.

Jeff ran.

He ran past the end of the bus, past the flaming barrels and decrepit possessions of a vagrant who'd claimed to be Carolina's son and the spawn of a school. Past the shattered remains of what had once been baseball practice nets, their chain-link trusses red with rust. He ran past small buildings he could not remember standing during the time he had worked here. He ran past rows of dumpsters. He ran past more gym equipment and even more lockers. He ran until a tangible stitch developed in his side. Finally he entered a hallway of a building, another narrow nerve center for a bank of classrooms. Reaching down, he felt for the familiar protuberance of his pistol ... and wasn't surprised to find it missing.

'Fucker,' he whispered. Having also pocketed his flashlight, there was nothing to see here but the ashen outline of wall-mounted lockers, the vague impression of classroom doors.

Motherfucking gun must have sprung out during the sprint. Only way to retrieve it is to retrace your steps.

But there was no way he was doing that. It would be like trying to locate a diamond in the rough, a needle in a freaking haystack. And a murdering son of a whore was now on the loose. A murderer who was not above matricide, of all things.

You really believe that was her son? More than likely that was a collective insanity ...

Watching the exchange, this had been Jeff's overriding thought: that everything leading up to their encounter by the school bus – the tales told, the desolate atmosphere *in which* they had been told – had all coalesced into a strange species of communal hysteria. One where their stories were made manifest. The vagrant had been nothing more than just that: a vagrant. Carolina had somehow misread his words, appropriated them to her own twisted mythology.

And now she's dead.

Despite looking into her vacant eyes and ruined stomach, this was the one thing Jeff had trouble processing. Everything about this night had reeked of *fiction* –

everything from Dillion filming proceedings like a carrion bird to each part of Providence Place that was comparable to the set of a movie. That Carolina Gates lay cooling was something his conscious mind struggled to grasp. Any second now, Dillion would enter this dark hallway accompanied by the others. Each of them would be grinning. *We got you a good one, didn't we, Jeff? That was some awesome footage of you running away ...*

Knowing the gun was gone did not waylay the prying of his fingers: they continued to scratch the lining of his trench coat as if by touch alone they could summon it. His other hand had found his completely useless cell phone. The phone was his secret shame because his pensioner's salary made no room for monetary credit on what was a pre-paid device. Mainly he carried the damn thing around for show because everybody else had one. Oftentimes in company he would peer at it, pretending to be on social media when all the while –

Emergency numbers are free. How did your old man's head brain-fart that fact?

A flood of relief pouring over him, Jeff pulled the cell phone out, almost spilling it twice in his excitement. Thumbing the side button, he breathed heavily while waiting for the familiar blue screen to light up, for the blessed bars to phase into existence ...

There was nothing. He kept pressing, shaking the plastic as if motion alone could awaken the battery. He swore again, something far cruder than fucker, the kind of curse his long dead mother would have berated him for, and that was when he heard the child's laughter from further down the hallway.

Now his breathing stopped entirely. When the sound came again, a flush of pure apprehension flooded his system.

The laughter of a young girl.

It drifted over again, and this time there was no mistaking it: laughter, almost mocking in the particulars. And not the kind of mirth one would attribute to wry amusement or fun. There was a devilish lilt, as if the girl was scornful of Jeff's predicament.

As if the girl was no younger than a teen.

TEN

Jason's sprint from the school bus also contained many obstacles, all of them like points in a maze leading back to one final destination. During the initial few seconds after Carolina fell backward he remembered Alyssa running by his side … but then she too disappeared when another shot erupted, jack-knifing away to the left like a sprung rabbit. At first his course had been a reverse trajectory of the route they had taken to reach the rear of Providence Place (he distinctly remembered bypassing the swing set in front of the theater), but then everything had dovetailed into a mish-mash of unrecognizable forms, all of them holding the stark attributes of a dream, the school only a flying facsimile of a true one.

The church had always been his destination.

Seeing it bleed out of the shadows he should have been surprised … but of course he wasn't. This was the final terminus all along, the endpoint he had never truly left; a physical *and* figurative altar calling him back for almost

two decades. Only slowing down as he reached the front
façade, Jason almost collapsed to the cement with a feeling
that had nothing to do with exhaustion. This was more akin
to doom; a fatalistic sense of defeat and the ultimate
despair.

Did you ever think you could leave? Kristin said in his
ear. *That Providence Place would just let you walk out now
after everything you've seen?*

No, he supposed he hadn't. Before leaving to meet the
others tonight he recalled going through a series of rituals
that had, in their uncanny way, resembled an altar boy's
mass preparations. He remembered cleaning out his food
pantry and disposing what was left in there; he remembered
scrubbing the floor tiles, walls, and finally the kitchen area
as if arranging for some kind of inspection or –

*Arranging things with the sure knowledge you would
never return.*

Dear God was *that* what he'd been doing? Making his
little apartment suitable for whoever had to follow in his
wake? It's what people often did before taking their leave
on a long vacation.

Or what they did before leaving the world altogether.

*Get out now, Jason. Your Honda is just behind you
through the front gates, sitting patiently all this time. Just
get out now and don't look back.*

Yes, he thought he could do that. But first he would
call for assistance. Carolina was dead. And the others …
where were they now? Had the vagrant found them also,
hunted them down in the same manner he did those
obscene animals who scoured this land?

Not taking his eyes from the church for even a second,

Jason reached down to feel the familiar bulge of his phone. It was there and accounted for, thank God. He should have taken it out sooner, should have called the police in the art rooms when –

'*Jason.*'

He froze. From the entrance of the gloomy interior, a voice had called to him. A voice almost certainly not that of Dillion or the others.

'*Jason,*' it repeated.

Though the voice had an authoritative air, it also came equipped with kindness. Its pitch seemed to demand submission, but it was peppered with enough gentility one felt powerless against it. Because kindness was a rare attribute these days. Teachers certainly didn't carry it, and neither did parents.

But there was another commanding figure who did.

He carried around kindness like a cape, this figure, coming to provide help just when you needed it, offering to soothe worried nerves armed only with the sound of his voice.

And the word of his God.

Phone completely forgotten now, Jason watched in hapless fascination as Father Parrington strode out of the darkness to greet him.

ELEVEN

Alyssa tripped upon seeing the swing-set, her whole body sprawling in a loose knot at the base of the closest one. Pain, sharp and smelling of wood chippings, crawled up her buttocks and midsection before settling into her wrists. Having used them to cushion her fall, dark scratches of blood were already materializing where splinters had broken through. For a full minute she simply lay there, inert, gritting her teeth against the pain ... though her ears remained pricked for the sound of pursuit. Trying to pin down coherent thought was waylaid by the impossible reality she had returned to the theater. Returned, despite the fact Alyssa had been running in the opposite direction from the man with the shotgun.

Returned? You've been unceremoniously dumped at its fucking feet.

Alyssa laughed into the woodchips, hands held out before her like claws. About three feet away stood the small dark silhouette of her backpack, jettisoned sometime during freefall and landing only a short distance away. Of course, there was nothing inside that could offer her any kind of comfort ... or be used as any kind of weapon against what she knew was coming.

From the doorway came the sound of hinges, squeaking on ancient brackets as the door itself swung open. Inside appeared a shaft of yellow light, weak at first but gaining strength with every inch the door opened. Pushing herself up by the elbows, Alyssa managed to leverage her body into a sitting position – then gradually stood up, kicking away shards of wood-chipping as if they were fattened leeches attached to her skin. She stared at the door, trying to muster the impetus to retreat.

Of which there is still time. A final showdown with Sadie Whitmore does not have to play out. Surely that's the kind of thing reserved for the screen? In real life, the heroine slinks back to the shadows to tend their wounds – with no begrudging audience to demand something more satisfying for the climax.

But who was she kidding here? Alyssa had been devoted to the theater, first acting in stage plays, then giving her greatest performance yet as *the girl trapped in a closet and forced to endure the frightful antics of a vengeful ghost.* Which meant there was no escaping where her final scenes would play out ... even if the director was no longer around to shoot them. Time and time again a narrative was given its overriding symmetry by coming full circle, to the place where everything had begun. It was, as some often said in the business, the nature of any three-act chronicle.

Bypassing her backpack without picking it up, Alyssa walked back into the theater of Providence Place.

TWELVE

Dillion Cook was lost.

How such a thing could happen – becoming lost in a place he had committed to memory – somehow defied logic. But lost he had become. Though everything was recognizable (classrooms, hallways, and courtyards), none of it was. Somehow another school had slipped over the veneer of this one, transforming Providence Place into an underworld labyrinth choking with horrors.

Horrors only visible through the plate-glass screen of his iPhone.

Every now and then his naked eye would alight on something – the crooked shadow of a man's crouched form, the sharp angle of a child's blazer – but the illusion would quickly evaporate, nothing firm in its place except the ruin of another deserted corridor. His camera, however, teemed with another world slowly coming to life, of people and creatures that had, up until now, been the sole domain of confessions by a battered and beleaguered cast.

His cast.

And just where were they now? Where were his actors when he needed them the most? Cowards, every last one of them. Running away at the first sign of real trouble.

(did Carolina really get shot or did I imagine that?)

and deserting their director. They didn't seem to understand making a film, any kind of film, was war. And what came with war? Casualties.

For a while Dillion had wandered, shouting out their names until his throat was hoarse. And during this time he never stopped filming, brandishing his smartphone around at the unseen world like a talisman. When the phone itself had begun showcasing things he could not perceive, Dillion had taken this as a sign from up high to keep moving and recording, actors be damned.

If Providence Place wants a witness, a scribe, then I will happily oblige.

The horrors were subtle to begin with – more dog-like creatures flitting through the viewfinder before Dillion could focus on them properly – then they evolved into something much grander: shining orbs moving with the lazy grace of a cloud and containing a peristaltic white so bright it was like looking into the nucleus of a star. From those orbs, bodies had sprouted. Malformed physiques with arms, legs, and grotesque heads contained within the framework of a writhing torso. When moving, they scuttled, darting over the concrete in the obscene manner of crabs. Though seemingly aware of Dillion's presence as he walked, they paid him no mind, moving quickly from one building to the next as though anxious to be joined to some unseen queen. At any other time such sights would have been a cause for alarm, but Dillion was too enamored by the spectacle to feel any fear. This kind of spectral activity wasn't merely going to make his film a success, it also had the potential to change the world. Because an *unseen* world was everywhere, and Dillion Cook could be the architect of its disclosure.

But only if I can find a way out ...

The more he walked, the more he failed to recognize what had come before. Familiar buildings had given way to archaic stone edifices whose blackened and bricked façades were creeping with trailing plants. Corridors had been replaced by pathways resembling the subsections of a graveyard. In the classrooms, moldering chairs and desks were being submitted to further dissolution, every inch of their bodies encased in a lime fungus which continued to grow the more it devoured.

Soon tangible sounds entered the fray: the din of a thousand children seeming to scream and laugh simultaneously. Every now and then he heard his own name spoken in the cacophony, like the low murmur of exchanged gossip whispered behind closed hands. Urging him to come forward, to keep filming, and witness a world that had only ever been abandoned by the living.

THIRTEEN

Despite no longer holding any source of light, Jason could discern the priest's square-cut features and three-day growth as if they had been granted a brightness all of their own. Garbed in a black vestment (the very same he'd sported on the day of his final mass), and clasping a leather-bound prayer book, Father Parrington was no longer afflicted by the diseases that had plagued him in life. Smiling almost demurely as he approached, he appeared more substantial than the backdrop of the church behind him, more colorful and real than the courtyard itself.

'Hello, Jason,' he said. Father Parrington's voice was cheerful, almost robust. Stopping just a few short feet away, he even deigned to rock back and forth on his heels. 'Beautiful night, isn't it? I'm so glad you made it back.'

Jason could feel his heart thumping below his neck like something caught. Yet his familiar coping mechanisms (either succumbing to anxiety or praying), had failed to materialize. And just why was that, exactly? Why, when during all his time under Father Parrington's tutelage he had felt a deep sense of unease? Both *before* the malady of his madness and after the man had surrendered to it. Part of it was the halo of disquiet all priests seemed to carry around with them; another part was perhaps the man's unfulfilled desires that were just as transparent as his vestments. No, Jason hadn't panicked yet because ...

'You're not really Father Parrington,' he said, a statement.

The priest nodded, satisfied. Still smiling, he said, 'You're a smart one, Jason Wedle. And that's why I've chosen you over the others. Oh, strength of character is one thing – your friend Alyssa has that in abundance, does she not? But strength of character pales in comparison to genuine intelligence. No, Jason, I am not Father Parrington. I am what you might call the headmaster of Providence Place.'

Swallowing in preparation to speak had become difficult, a herculean task. He said, 'You chose me?'

That brief nod of the head again, like someone holding in a laugh.

'To palaver, of course. To discuss among ourselves what your presence here means. And what, exactly, comes next. Not just for you, Jason, but for *all* of you. You five bright souls who have, on this dark night, chosen to call Providence Place home.'

Jason felt something sliding into place, unanswered questions illuminated like a puzzle solved. From their first moments together as a group standing inside the decay of the main courtyard, each returning pilgrim had felt (and sometimes articulated), the presence of a shadow behind the curtain: the unseen architect of Providence Place pulling at the strings. They had all witnessed Carolina's dark cloud, of course; had even heard the scream of something not-quite-human shrieking its mournful tune. But these had only been slivers of the sub-rosa phantom; foot soldiers for a form of energy composed of nothing but appetite.

Here stood that energy, guised as a memory, but somehow all the more potent for that.

'What do you want?' he asked the school. For now there could be little doubt who he was addressing.

When the headmaster grinned this time, parts of his human façade appeared to slough off; the bulge of his cheek almost rubbery as it moved; the whitened teeth exhibiting corruption.

'Why, for you to make a decision, Jason. For you to decide your fate tonight.

FOURTEEN

Like a man in a dream, Jeff Wolfe moved toward the sound of laughter.

Marcy Ribald's teasing laughter.

It's just her ghost, old man. That's no more her real laugh than anything else you've seen tonight.

The corridor ended, and a new one began. Every time another set of classrooms presented themselves, the laughter grew louder. Yet each time he came within inches of exposing it, the sound would drift away again. On and on this pattern went until Jeff, half-maddened by its echo, began calling out the names of Dillion, Alyssa, and Jason – hoping his entreaties would give this aimless wandering some kind of compass point. Then, knowing full-well the potential harm he invited, Jeff finally began to give voice to the name of Marcy Ribald, spitting out the syllables of his lifelong torment like a maligned curse and daring her to step out into the light.

Soon, his pleas were answered.

FIFTEEN

A full house.

Alyssa gazed out at a sea of faces, dozens of rictus-grin smiles leering back at the stage. Though the spotlight above had pinned its beam on her the second she'd alighted the stage, Alyssa could still see the faces of the audience like grim and expectant bobbleheads awaiting her next move.

The spotlight was my anchor ...

Yes, it was; Alyssa remembered this distinctly. Always, she had traversed from one scene to another in any given performance because the spotlight managed to expunge the ogling eyes of a crowd. It was easy to pretend you were living in a fantasy world when each spectator stood veiled behind the black armband of an artificial smokescreen. This was her secret weapon. An ace up the sleeve and one of the main reasons she never flailed when others did. But now Alyssa could see their faces all too clearly ... and some of them were familiar.

In the backrow sat Edith Kerrigan and Debra Harrison,

two sophomores who had perished in a car accident while Alyssa was still in middle school. Next to them was a small man sporting a moustache, a red baseball cap, and a face lined with wrinkles like ingrown blackheads. David Fassett, a Providence Place groundskeeper run over by one of his own tractors. Though she barely recalled the man, she *did* recall the memorial held in his wake, a by-the-numbers sendoff for the grieving students and faculty. Mr. Fassett's smiling picture had been strung up around the church like a collage of missing person's posters. The groundskeeper's grisly demise had been one of her first ever brushes with death. At least until –

Whitmore. Sadie Whitmore. And here she is now in the front row, complete with a ravaged neck and dead eyes. She's holding something in her bone-white hands, something she tried giving you in the dressing rooms all those long years ago: a perfect noose fit for the gallows. Are you ready to wear it now, Alyssa, as you surely should have from the start? Are you ready to give your final performance?

SIXTEEN

While the headmaster talked, Jason bore witness to the
true nature of Providence Place.

Abandoned and derelict in the present, the school was
not so in whatever unimaginable timescale it thrived in.
Human beings, semi-transparent for the most part,
negotiated the courtyards and buildings like lost souls
seeking paradise. Although some wore the astringent attire
befitting teachers and heads of staff, most bore the blazers
and bags of young children. Some walked; others jogged.
Some were holed up in stairwells, staring out at nothing.
One thing was similar about all of them: a forlorn
expression of misery; of something eternally misplaced.
They would never leave, these children. Never know the
sweet sound of a bell signifying home.

Like insects caught in amber, Providence Place had
pinioned their secret selves.

Hell is repetition, Jason thought.

The school said, 'You have a decision to make, Jason.'

How did everything come to this? he wondered.

What kind of God would allow something so sinister to give him such an ultimatum? Providence Place wanted more emotions, where the creature called *human* could be manipulated and given a taste of pure burning appetite. Not just emotions, either; it wanted Jason to go back into the real world and pioneer the seeds of its resurrection, to bring about a return of human activity and commotion.

All Jason had to do was agree, and his life would be spared.

'What will happen to the others?' he asked.

The headmaster's face contorted, ripples of rot giving glimpses of the disease festering beneath. 'My son will finish what he started.'

SEVENTEEN

She emerged from the shadows dressed for the occasion: short blue skirt and halter top, jet-black hair pinned back in a ponytail. It was the same outfit she wore every night during her shift; the same outfit worn when deciding to butcher numerous students then perform an act of self-mutilation so visceral in the particulars it was almost beyond the measure of understanding.

She's chewing gum, too, Jeff thought. *I'll be damned.*

Her smile was seductive; her waltz equally so. When she chewed, it was with the lewd abandon of the promiscuous. Edging closer, the lockers to either side of them bled away to nothing. Darkness receded, and a natural glow took its place.

'You lied before, didn't you, Mr. Wolfe?' Marcy said to him.

'Lied?'

'Back in the closet, when you told your story,' Marcy sniggered, running a hand through her ponytail. 'I was *listening.'*

'You were?'

Marcy nodded, a roguish smile curling the side of her lip. 'Of course. And you didn't just lie, but you left parts of the story out, didn't you? You left out the part where after you caught me with Regina, you went home and jerked yourself off.'

This isn't Marcy, he told himself. *It's just the motherfucking unseen world.*

That might be so … but the illusion was solid. Jeff could even smell her perfume, the caustic aroma of something cheap. Black nail polish on the tips of her fingers gleamed as though recently applied.

And let's not forget her words are essentially true. Jeff Wolfe, a poor cleaner who lived alone, whose sole outlet when it came to sexual gratification entailed watching porn, had indeed jerked his wad at the end of that long day. Though who could blame him? He was a lonely man, and –

'But it wasn't just that night, either, was it, Mr. Wolfe?' said Marcy, now edging closer with each word. 'You thought about me often, didn't you? Right from the very beginning. Thought about putting it inside of me in the cleaning closet after lights out. Just the two of us, yes? That was your fantasy. You thought you could show me the ropes – an experienced old man and a younger woman. You would *teach* me.'

Those nail-polish adorned fingers … Jeff watched as Marcy slipped one of them into the top of her skirt, watched her push it underneath the hem. All the while still moving, making small, skittish steps and holding him with her gaze. Not just chewing the gum, now. But *gnawing* on it.

'Get back,' he said, the words sounding somehow pathetic. 'Or I'll ...'

'You'll what, Mr. Wolfe? What will you do? What do you *want* to do to me? We have all the time in the world, now. The headmaster will see to it.'

Despite the incongruity of the moment Jeff raised his head, curious. 'Headmaster?' he asked.

'He wants you to stay, Jeff. You and some of the others.'

So close now he could reach out and touch her if he wanted. And did he want to? *Oh God, yes.* Never wavering from their intent, Marcy's fingers had found that sweet portion of her underneath the hem's lining, and there they began to knead. He thought back to the hundreds of times his mind had played out a scenario very close to this one: being seduced, forcefully, by Marcy or one of his other young coworkers. And now the opportunity was presenting itself; his ultimate dream made manifest.

And what does the world outside these walls have to offer an ageing nigger, anyway? Nothing but a shitty apartment, a lousy pension, and a limp dick. You can also add dementia to the list ... because only a senile old fool would believe some cheap-ass film would've made them a star.

Sensing his realization dawning, Marcy's eyes brightened. And in that glint Jeff noticed something move. A shadow; something's elongated reflection. Yet a thing substantial enough to break his reverie entirely. Suddenly the illusion shattered, and Marcy's form became the elusive nothing it had surely been from the start.

Slowly turning around, Jeff had time to comprehend a blur of hulking silhouette

(*oh God, Maddox*)

and the abyss of a muzzle before Providence Place and everything in it was plunged back into darkness.

EIGHTEEN

First wearing out the battery of one iPhone, Dillion replaced it with another. And then a third. The more he witnessed, the more power his lithe little cameras seemed to consume. As if the scenery were full of pixels, and he had only been allocated a certain amount of software. Vaguely aware there had once been others by his side, that particular adventure now seemed a lifetime ago. In its place was the bourgeoning empire of the ancient, unseen world … one whose sheer profundity of forms defied adequate description. In addition to the wandering orbs, other configurations of regressive life had wandered into the viewfinder. Things with glistening eyes attached to buttocks and hides composed of nothing but teeth. Itinerant, the teeth would produce liquid chattering sounds, while the eyes wept and disgorged fat yellow discharge that pooled around twitching limbs like the appendages of a quartered and struggling caterpillar. Dillion filmed, and kept filming, and after a time the other, older world began to reassert itself once again; the grey world of barren hallways and empty classrooms; a world where humans had been driven out by the ghosts of their own banal appetite.

Exiting a block of buildings, familiar sights came to greet Dillion: serried ranks of yellow school buses and the fragrant reek of wood smoke; crumbling concrete containing a ceiling of serpentine fog like a thin atmosphere.

Separated from the pack, errant and misguided, sat a school bus having the attributes of a derelict home …

Suddenly everything came crashing back: Maddox, now a grown-up vagrant, had shot his mother. And Dillion had caught it on camera. Matricide for the masses. Then he had run, and so had the others, and then …

Lowering his phone, Dillion made his way over toward the bus. Makeshift fires from the barrels continued to cast the scene in a ruddy glow … but there was another source of light, one that had followed him ever since he'd fled this scene – a chalky, flat radiance highlighting corners and coating the asphalt like the ebb and whorl of an Etch A Sketch. Although no stars were visible, fat columns of spectral cloud gave off their own sickly shine. By the illumination, he could make out the plump oblong of a sprawled and lifeless body. *Carolina's* body. So he hadn't imagined the whole thing, after all. His movie really did have a climactic murder. And there was something else, as well … some other thing lying a few feet away next to the rear tires of the bus. Another lifeless body, this one sprawled on its stomach.

That can't be right – everyone got away. Didn't they?
Curiosity piqued, Dillion's slow walk became a trot.

Then a small sprint. Though aware Maddox could be lurking anywhere (could in fact have his shotgun trained from one of the bus's windows), finding out the identity of the second body was suddenly paramount.

Almost tripping over some of Maddox's refuse (an encrusted mattress and skinned carcasses), Dillion stumbled into the pall of light created by the ebbing barrel fires. And yes ... here was Carolina, her printed flower dress soaked with gore and her right hand still clutching her flashlight. In the livid light, her skin had the complexion of blood-soaked beef; her eyes like the jellied fat on a cooling dinner cadaver. Her mouth, much like the corpse in the stairwell, had frozen in a silent scream. Without pausing to think about it, Dillion lifted up his iPhone ... but stopped short when his eyes again alighted on the second body beside the tires.

Shot in the back. And wearing a long-sleeved designer shirt with faded jeans.

The kind of thing a devil-may-care director would possibly don. Doc Martins completed the ensemble.

Dillion's world doubled, then trebled. Pitching forward, he only just managed to keep his balance, coming to rest less than a foot from the body. Although the face was only partially visible, Dillion didn't need to see it all to know there would be a small white scar running along the base of the chin ... the end result of a bicycle accident at the age of twelve. Just as he didn't need to see underneath the bloody shirt to know there was a small tattoo of Tarantino on the left abdomen, a permanent reminder that it was possible to create motherfucking art with nothing but unwavering ambition.

The dead body was Dillion Cook.

I never got away, he thought.

Memories of the unseen world were suddenly filling him up, relentless and assaulting: Carolina's dark cloud infected with a city of faces. And inside that maelstrom a fresh countenance newly added to the fray – *his* face.

Filled with the agony of an impending eternity inside the walls of Providence Place.

NINETEEN

From the gallows, a single noose beckoned.

Watching on, a ratchet of applause went up from the audience of ghosts, all of them cheering wildly. Though the auditorium was now filled with the sounds of mirth, the spectators producing the revelry were a catalogue of death and disfigurement: rotting faces and marble eyes. For every person Alyssa recognized, there were at least a dozen more she did not.

Men, women ... but mostly children.

Just like the ones in the mirror.

What had she been thinking, coming back here? In the time between her last day of school and Dillion's proposition, a species of *forgetfulness* had taken root, her time under this roof something of no more substance than one of her plays. Even when recounting her story for Dillion's camera, her episode in the dressing rooms had felt like an actor's scenes. Only now was she recalling how utterly *cloying* and *claustrophobic* the whole experience had been. A haunting to end them all. And yet in the aftermath of the ordeal, Alyssa Asterious had simply gone on with her life and relegated Sadie Whitmore to the shadows.

But Sadie had never forgotten her.

She stood by the gallows, fawning over the solitary noose like a game-show hostess indicating a prize. Standing here earlier, a kind of torpor had infiltrated her body, and now Alyssa felt the same inertia take hold again, guiding her inside the gallows. As more applause erupted, Alyssa noticed additional bodies added to the tapestry of grinning clown faces ... the faces of Carolina, Jeff, and Dillion. No longer incumbent to life, they cheered on with the same wild-eyed abandon as the rest of the dead, urging Alyssa ever onward. In Carolina's abdomen, a gaping hole told the tale of her demise. In Jeff's left eye, the same. Only Dillion seemed unscathed ... but then she saw the red flower that was his back, a stygian wound from shoulder blade to buttocks.

Where's Jason? she had time to think. *Did he somehow get away –*

But then one of Sadie's hands gripped her own, tugging her forward. Before slipping the noose over her head, Alyssa was given one last glimpse into those fathomless black eyes ... and saw nothing in them but the roving forms of Providence Place, of power with appetite finally gaining back what was once denied.

TWENTY

Inside the carpark, Jason's Honda sat unharmed, a bright red counterpoint against the charcoal dark. Although dawn was nearing, no daylight could be seen peeking over the horizon.

The cars belonging to Dillion and Alyssa had vanished. *Never to return*, he thought randomly. *The headmaster has seen to it.*

Feeling himself shudder, Jason turned around to peer back at Providence Place. From this perspective, there was no sign of the force that had occupied Father Parrington or of the unseen world; only the bricks and mortar of something deserted and left to die.

But Providence Place will not die. Not if it has its way with me.

Jason had returned seeking closure, a chance to put aside or even close the books on Providence Place forever. Instead, the school had tasked him with homework, and now he would never be free of her walls or the creatures that dwelled inside.

Not if he wanted to go on living.

Facing away, Jason walked back to his car.

Although an opaque mist clung to the undersides of the Honda, this did not prevent him from seeing the objects placed only a few feet away from the tires as he inched closer: small articles rectangular in shape and arranged in a neat pile for Jason to discover.

I'll help you, the headmaster had said. A rejoinder when Jason had put forth the question as to how *he* could possibly assist in ushering life back into Providence Place. Well, here was that help: three of their director's iPhones containing everything that had transpired on this night. Every word; every reaction; every dark happening showing itself to the pilgrims. Jason Wedle was now free to create an entirely new movie of his own, one that would bring a tide of flesh back to the unseen world.

To live, I play the Devil's emissary.

Bending down, Jason picked up Dillion's phones. Then he got in his car and drove away.

TWENTY-ONE

Through the darkness of Providence Place, someone moves from room to room, a man of middle age and a scion of the school.

Coming to rest in a classroom containing mannequins, the man lights a solitary match.

For a while the flame simply stutters, as if the hand holding it only desires to observe light for its own sake. Then the match is dropped, first igniting mildewed sheets underfoot before catching onto the vermin.

There is a cacophony of shrieks, followed by silence. The sound is repeated on and on until sitting mannequins also catch the conflagration.

His mother returning was just the beginning.

Soon, he would greet the arrival of others. And when they came, the man would help usher in the penultimate fire; a fire to end them all and a purging of the world itself.

TWENTY-TWO

From *The Cranston Herald*:

EX STUDENT TO REOPEN LOCAL SCHOOL
WITH CHRISTIAN INTERACTIVE EXPERIENCE.

In what comes as a surprise to many, the long defunct
Cranston school, Providence Place, has found a developer
for the 12-acre site. Once a vital piece of infrastructure
within the residential area, Providence Place was plagued
by a list of tragedies that led to the school's foreclosure in
2004. Noted for its intricate brick and stonework cornice,
the school has since fallen into disrepair. In more recent
years, Providence Place developed a sinister reputation,
carrying the title of haunted, becoming the focal point of
tabloid fodder and interstate ghost hunters.

Jason Wedle, local zealous Christian and once a student of

Providence Place, has plans for a themed 'hell-house experience' described on the ticket sales page as featuring 'life or death moral choices where guests would receive in-your-face scenes of dark reality. You will walk the school and encounter individuals who will make choices. The choice is life or death; sin or salvation; Heaven or Hell.'

The Rhode Island Public School System told *The Cranston Herald* the controversial event will not take place on the site, and a complaint has been lodged with the City of Cranston. A spokesperson said that despite these 'Hell Houses' being popular among some evangelical Christian groups, they are strongly opposed to anyone benefitting from the dark history of Providence Place.

The Craston Herald reports that a casting call for the event posted to Facebook last month described it as a 'Christian Interactive Experience' and specifically sought out former students for some of its scenes.

Despite recently receiving hate mail, the director is unrepentant.

'They have stipulated it is offensive,' Jason wrote. 'But we are working very hard on this production, trying to shed light on the truth of the world.'

February 2016 – November 2016
Adelaide, South Australia.

ABOUT THE AUTHOR

A vociferous columnist in horror circles since 2005, Matthew Tait published his first collection of dark fiction in 2011. Since then he has been nominated for the prestigious Shadows Award in the category of novel and gone on to publish an illustrated book of non-fiction. Described as writing 'the sort of horror Clive Barker must read on his days off,' Matthew's fiction often treads the line between the familiar and the fantastic. His latest book, *Olearia*, is the second novel in an epic trilogy of dark fantasy.